MAYERLING

CLAUDE ANET

MAYERLING

The Love and Tragedy of a Crown Prince

UNABRIDGED

PAN BOOKS LTD : LONDON

First published 1930 by Hutchinson & Co (Publishers) Ltd.

Published 1968 by Leslie Frewin Publishers Ltd.

This edition published 1968 by Pan Books Ltd.,
33 Tothill Street, London, S.W.1

330 02212 1

*Printed and bound in England by
Hazell Watson and Viney Ltd
Aylesbury, Bucks*

CONTENTS

PART I

PART II

PART III

MAYERLING

PART I

PROLOGUE

A LARGE ROOM, luxuriously furnished, with a lofty ceiling, and two windows looking down on to a park with stately trees. A young woman lay on a bed partly screened from the remainder of the room. Stretched out on the pillow, the coils of her thick plaits of chestnut hair formed a sort of halo. Her face, though drawn with pain, was beautiful; her mouth was shapely; she had exquisitely pencilled straight dark brows. From time to time a moan escaped her lips, and she could be seen to twist in pain beneath her covering.

At her bedside was a group of watchful attendants: an old man wearing a frock coat with decoration; a younger man with a clever face, in a white coat; and two nurses, and, at the time when a woman, racked in body and mind, has the right to be alone, several other people were gathered near. Elisabeth of Austria belonged to a caste which permitted neither joy nor pain to be kept hidden. At the age of twenty, she was about to be confined; not even under these delicate circumstances was privacy permitted.

At one of the windows of this room stood His Imperial and Royal Highness, the Archduke Rainer, Prime Minister of the Empire, a little old man on tottering legs. He was conversing in low tones with a privy councillor, Charles Ferdinand, Count Buel Schauenstein. Three other personages in uniform looked silently out into the park with its straight avenues, where night was falling. Two ladies sat whispering in a corner. A man of scarcely thirty, in the dark green uniform of a general of Uhlans, was leaning upright against the mantelpiece. He was of average height, slim, long-legged, his face set in a frame of long fair whiskers and a heavy moustache, his hair cut short and getting thin over the temples, his nose rather thick at the end, his eyes without much expression. Notwithstanding his great self-control – and his life during the last ten years as Emperor of Austria and King of Hungary had taught him to master and conceal his feelings – he was unable to hide his nervousness, which he betrayed by cracking the fingers of his right hand over the joints of his left hand. At times he became aware of it, stopped suddenly, and, tugging furiously at his moustache, strode over to the window, causing his boots to creak on the floor. At last the noise irritated the Empress, and she signed to him to keep still.

He stopped at once.

'I beg your pardon, darling,' he murmured.

And on tiptoe, like a child who has been reproved, he returned to the mantelpiece.

An hour passed thus. The room grew dark, and the constraint of the assembled company became almost unbearable. Each of those present felt he was taking part, not in a ceremony, but in a most poignant human drama. The court dresses and uniforms seemed to offer insult to the frail woman quivering beneath the sheet which covered her. The silence was broken only by the more frequent moans of the sufferer. At times the Emperor, still standing by the mantelpiece, could not restrain his restlessness. Lackeys in embroidered coats unconcernedly brought lighted candlesticks, the flames of which sent sparkles into the diamonds of the decorations, and threw a flickering light on the gilded wainscoting.

There was a stir among the doctors at the bedside. Professor Baldensperger leaned over the Empress, who was suffering her last pangs; a moment passed, then a louder moan caused a shudder among the witnesses of this dramatic scene; the Emperor, unable to endure it any longer, uttered a 'Mein Gott', as if in supplication, and buried his head in his hands. There was a scream, then silence, so complete that each one could feel the beating of his heart, and suddenly was heard a puling cry, so natural, so human, and so unexpected that the eyes of those present filled with tears.

'It's a boy!' announced Dr Herrenschmidt, in his resonant voice.

'Praise be to God!' responded the Emperor.

While the doctors busied themselves behind the screen, the doors of the adjoining room were thrown wide open and the joyful news was made known. The Christian name chosen for the Heir-Apparent was announced. He was to be called Rudolph, in honour of the founder of the thousand-year-old dynasty of the Hawks, who had deserted the forests of Switzerland and had come to hover about the fair land of Austria. An hour later, after the new-born babe had been preliminarily baptized, and the birth duly registered and dated August 21st, 1858, there remained no one at the castle of Laxenbourg but the physicians and the officials of the court on duty.

The Empress asked for her infant. He had just been bathed, and the nurse brought him to her, wrapped in warm flannels.

For long the Empress gazed at him. He was so frail that he seemed destined not to live. The hours she had just passed came back to her memory. Such pomp and circumstance, so many conflicting interests about her – and here was her babe, puny and defenceless. Fresh terrors harassed the suffering mother, as she felt the heritage of the past bear heavily upon her infant son. He belonged to a highly strung, impressionable race, unable to bear the burden of power or even of life, which had produced beings of unbalanced mind, unequal to their destiny, and whose feet folly had sometimes led astray off the beaten human track. What kind of gift had she made to this weak mortal in giving him birth? One day tremendous responsibilities would weigh heavily upon him. He would be crushed beneath them. At that moment the approaching footsteps of the Emperor were heard. He leaned over his wife and their child, and said, in impressive tones:

'He is splendid, our little son. What a happy fellow he will be!'

But the mother's eyes filled with tears; she took her baby in her arms and pressed him passionately to her breast.

CHAPTER I

THE CROWN PRINCE

THIRTY YEARS LATER, on a glorious Spring morning, an
officer was cantering a thoroughbred along an avenue of the
Prater. Despite his youthful appearance, he wore the undress
uniform of a cavalry general. On reaching the end of the
avenue he put his horse into a walk. He was slim, well-pro-
portioned, of medium height, with fine eyes and a long
moustache. He acknowledged, with an easy grace, the deferential salutations of other riders who passed him.

He dismounted at the spot where the main avenue meets a
square fringed with houses, known as the Star of the Prater.
He handed his horse over to a groom, and stood alone for a
moment on the footpath, waiting for his phaeton. Presently,
he caught sight of it on the other side of the square and
went to meet it.

Just at that moment some shop-girls came running out of
a milliner's establishment. One of them heedlessly ran into
him, and nearly fell. He caught her gently, set her on her
feet, gave her a pleasant smile, and went on his way. The
shop-girl looked at him with wonder in her eyes.

Meanwhile her companions made fun of her.

'So that's how you throw yourself into gentlemen's arms!'
they said.

But one of the older of them, following the officer with her
eyes, said to her reproachfully:

'Aren't you ashamed of yourself, Greta, jostling the Crown
Prince like that!'

The girls were all dumbfounded, and turned round to look
at their famous Viennese Prince. Could it really be he, who
had appeared in their midst, like a prince in a fairy story?
A few yards away, their hero was stepping into his phaeton,

and the groom was handing him the reins. The horses
pranced and were off. As the carriage skirted the footpath
where the girls stood staring, open-mouthed, the Prince
saluted. Some of them waved; all beamed at him merrily.

'How handsome he is! How kind!' they exclaimed.

*   *   *

'Is it for confession that you have come, Madame?'

The question was put by Father Bernsdorf, Father
Superior of the Jesuit College in Austria, to a rather tall lady,
of ungainly build, who was dressed without any great dis-
tinction. She was none other than Her Imperial and Royal
Highness, Stephanie, Crown Princess of Austria.

She was in the private room of Father Bernsdorf in the
Jesuit convent in the street of the Bernardins. The room was
whitewashed; its floor was of red bricks. It was sparsely furnished, containing nothing but a wooden table, two armchairs covered with rep, two cane-bottom chairs and a
praying-stool.

The Princess replied with a shade of embarrassment:

'No, Father, I have simply come to talk to you.'

She sat down in one of the armchairs, and motioned to
the Jesuit to take the other. Only the table separated them.

Presumably the matter the Princess wished to discuss with
the Jesuit was a delicate one, for she hesitated before broaching it. On noticing this, the priest came to her aid and led
the conversation up to the Crown Prince.

'Is the Crown Prince in good health?' he asked.

'He is overdoing it,' said the Princess. 'He will never stand
the strain. You see, he does everything with such ardour –
work, shooting and hunting. Every minute of his day is
filled.'

'His health is of vital importance to us all,' said the Jesuit.
'Could you not use your influence and get him to rest for an
hour or two?'

A pained look came into the Princess's face.

'I never see him,' she began.

She stopped abruptly, as if she regretted having spoken too hastily. The tone of this short sentence made the matter clear to the Jesuit. He showed no sign, however, and continued:

'Still, in the evenings—'

'In the evenings,' said the Princess, with embarrassment, 'we go out. If he takes me to the Opera or the Burg Theatre, he scarcely stays with me; he goes into the corridors or behind the scenes. After the theatre he has supper with friends. I am not invited, and for a very good reason.'

There was anger in the Princess's eyes, but the priest, following her train of thought, asked unconcernedly:

'And later?'

To this too pertinent question he received no answer. There remained one point to clear up, and after a few seconds he added:

'Has this been so for long?'

Again a pause, this time prolonged. The priest, who had been speaking with lowered eyes, now raised them. He saw before him an embarrassed woman, blushing and unable to look him in the face. At least a minute dragged on in silence. Finally the Princess spoke. Addressing herself to the table, she murmured:

'For a year.'

Despite his considerable self-command, the priest could not repress a movement. Discord in the Crown Prince's household – the thing was serious, the consequences incalculable. He must consider it calmly, and advise. When he spoke again, his voice betrayed no emotion.

'Why did you not speak to me sooner?' he asked.

'The matter was so delicate,' replied the Princess, still embarrassed. 'The position might have changed from one day to another. Nothing had happened, you see, to separate us. Every evening I thought that perhaps the Prince would return.'

The vehemence with which she uttered these words revealed her feelings towards her unfaithful husband.

'A year,' he repeated, shaking his head, 'a year. And how old is your little daughter, my child?'

It was the first time that he had addressed her thus on that day.

'She is just four, Father.'

The Jesuit reflected.

'You have done well in speaking to me,' he said at last. 'Perhaps you should have done so sooner. I share your anxieties. There is no heir to the throne— But the ways of God are inscrutable. At the hour God chooses, He will bring your husband back to you. God will not forsake this Empire, which is in His special keeping; I have proof of that. Patience is needed, my child. I know your feelings; you will know how to act as a Christian wife; you must give no sign of ill-feeling.' He slipped in this sentence almost imperceptibly. 'You will need much forbearance. You will thus prepare the way of God. And you must pray. Ah! There I can give you help.' His voice sounded strong and confident at the idea of the assistance he was bringing her. 'I shall order a novena,' he said, stressing each word, 'in all our colleges, with prayers that a son and heir may be born to the ancient House of Hapsburg.'

The Princess did not appear so grateful as he had expected for the support he offered. She thanked him, however, then added:

'I wanted to ask you, Father, to see the Prince and speak to him.'

The priest made a movement of nervousness.

'That is difficult, my child, extremely difficult.'

'Nothing is difficult for you,' continued the Princess.

'I should have to ask for an audience,' said the Jesuit, 'and state the purpose of the audience – I cannot say—'

'You would have no trouble in finding a motive for seeing the Prince,' she said. 'You know, as I do, the magnitude of the interests at stake.'

The priest reflected for a moment.

'You are right, my child,' he said. 'I will see the Prince.'

A few minutes later, the Princess and her lady-in-waiting got back into their carriage.

As Father Bernsdorf re-entered his room, he appeared to be wrapped in thought. 'A year,' he thought. 'A year already! Why didn't she tell me before? What woman is gaining influence over the Prince? He is weaker than I thought. What intrigues! What a network of pernicious influences! Has she already been supplanted?' He shrugged his shoulders. 'If there were anything serious, I should know. In any case I must see.'

*   *   *

The same day, about noon, two people were talking in a small room adjoining the editorial office of the *Neues Wiener Tageblatt*. One of them was Herr Szeps, the editor in chief of that paper, a thin man of medium height. Though he was by no means an old man, his close-cropped hair had turned white, his complexion was sallow. The only fleshy part of his bony face was the end of his nose, which had an unmistakably Jewish hook.

Well known as a journalist in Vienna, he edited with skill, in difficult times, a Liberal paper opposing the Conservative – not to say autocratic – government of Count Taafe. His colleagues and well-informed members of Government circles were constantly astonished at the accuracy of the information of his paper, and the unexpected news it sometimes contained on crucial political topics. But the articles were invariably couched in such unprovocative language that the Press Censor could never find a pretext for suspending the newspaper. 'Where the devil does Szeps get his information?' people wondered. This provided a problem which exercised the astutest minds, but no satisfactory solution had ever been reached.

So Szeps continued to enjoy a prestige and influence un-justified by the slender circulation of his paper. That day, there sat opposite him an old man and fellow Jew, Herr Blum, proprietor and manager of the above-mentioned news-paper, from whom he had no secrets.

As the two men were discussing, with the subtlety and relish for dialectics so congenial to the Jews, an intricate problem of Austro-Hungarian politics, the subject of the Emperor cropped up. 'There is,' they averred, 'no hope of improvement during his lifetime.'

'He's an old man,' said Szeps.

'He's only fifty-nine and may last another ten years,' replied Blum. 'He's not clever, and has no comprehension of the matters that interest us so intensely, but it's as well to recognize that, with such means as he has, he pursues his own course and gets his own way in spite of innumerable obstacles.'

'When he is gone,' said Szeps, 'he will leave such a mess behind him that the worst is bound to happen. We shall get a revolution with bloodshed, and a separatist movement that will break up the Empire. And when I think of that splendid son of his! Ah. Blum, never has Austria had a Crown Prince like him, and I rather think she is unworthy of him. In Rudolph we should at last see an Emperor suited to modern needs, and receptive of our own generous ideas. And what a future for Europe to look forward to! With Frederick III on the German throne, and Rudolph on the Austro-Hungarian, the parties of reaction would receive their death-blow throughout the world. Even Russia— What hopes it engenders, my dear Blum, but at the same time,' he lowered his voice, 'what fears! A marvellous prospect de-pendent on the life of one man! Meanwhile there is grave cause for anxiety; his married life is unhappy; he is continu-ally at loggerheads with his wife, who is a difficult woman, stubborn and, alas, without brain. What he needs above all is a restful home life, and constant affectionate support. In-stead, there are continual quarrels, the rumours of which find

a way through the thick walls of the Hofburg. The result?'
He lowered his voice again. 'The Prince drowns his troubles
in dissipation.'

Here Blum's hearty laugh interrupted him.

'Come, my friend, you needn't be so alarmed. Is he the
first heir to a throne to indulge in mild dissipations? The
wild youth of Henry V of England – he was a thousand
times wilder than Rudolph – did not prevent him from
being a great king. Plenty of others have done the same,
and many more will do so. It's not a bad training ground
for budding kings. It merely proves the Crown Prince to be
alive and full of spirit.'

'But it may end in a scandal,' rejoined Szeps, refusing to
be convinced.

At this Blum laughed louder than before.

'The masters of the Hofburg have nothing to learn in the
art of suppressing scandals. So let the Prince enjoy himself
in his own way, while he is young. *Gaudeamus igitur dum
juvenes sumus*,' chirped the old man. 'And, as we have
several ways of obtaining reliable information, we will take
good care no one dangerous becomes too intimate with him.
So long as he confines himself to taking pretty girls out to
supper, there will be no harm, but if a clever woman began
to get hold of him, we should have to see. He has never
mentioned his private life to you?'

'Never, nor do I wish it. That's dangerous ground, on
which I should be sorry to venture.'

'Still, try to find out something, if you get an opportunity.
When do you expect to see him?'

'He leaves for Budapest tomorrow. As soon as he returns,
he is to give me a rendezvous. How I enjoy these rendezvous
at the Hofburg, but how they scare me! Think of the fearful
hullabaloo if somebody met and recognized me! But the
Prince has his wits about him, and at every fresh meeting
I take extra precautions. Next time I shall be wearing black
glasses.'

CHAPTER II

THE HOFBURG

WHY IS THERE so often something depressing in the aspect of a royal palace? Is it due to an impersonal exterior, which gives no inkling of the life behind its walls, to the austere and monotonous effect of rows of lofty windows, or to the total absence of individuality? It is difficult to say. But the Hofburg, in which Rudolph lived and had been brought up, was perhaps the most dismal palace in Europe. All its apartments looked down upon vast courtyards, without a tree, a flower, or a piece of greenery to relieve the pervading gloom. So grey and silent was its atmosphere that even the cheeky Viennese sparrows would not venture to look for crumbs beneath its forbidding windows.

Nor was the everyday life of its august inhabitants such as to bring a note of gaiety or animation. The Emperor and Empress occupied two suites of apartments overlooking the courtyard known as Franzens Platz. The Emperor's suite, with its main entrance underneath the archway leading to the Michaeler Platz, comprised a series of rooms all decorated with white and gold woodwork, in the rococo style, and containing massive furniture in which gold predominated. In a corner of each room stood a huge earthenware stove, also in gold and white, which gave out an evenly regulated heat in winter. There was a room for the use of the aides-de-camp and two for receiving in audience exalted personages. In the Emperor's private office were two windows and two desks, at one of which he worked standing. His sleeping chamber had a narrow brass bed. There was one other salon in this wing with a row of windows facing south.

The Empress's apartments began at the right angle of the building. They were raised several feet above the Emperor's and connected with them by four stairs. Her sleeping chamber led into a reception-room, then came the salon of the ladies-in-waiting and the dining-room. All these rooms were furnished much more tastefully than the Emperor's, but were of such vast dimensions that even a profusion of flowers and plants gave them no touch of home likeness or animation. In the return wing were the apartments used for State receptions, and, finally, those reserved for the Archducal families and the Emperor's guests.

The Emperor was then fifty-eight. A life of unremitting toil had prematurely aged him. His hair was white; the front and top of his head were bald. His face was deeply lined, and his nose had thickened. He was, however, still active, for his limbs had retained their shapeliness, and he kept his bearing of a cavalryman. But he had developed into a confirmed bureaucrat. With a religious respect for the routine of business, which was smoothly and expeditiously transacted, he never referred to others matters that could be settled directly by himself. Retiring to bed early, he was at work before dawn, and Viennese revellers crossing the Franzens Platz in winter would see a light in the Emperor's apartments by five in the morning. At that hour a lamp was placed on Franz Joseph's desk, and the aide-de-camp on duty – who had perhaps come straight from a ballroom – was bending over the Emperor and receiving his orders for the day. In summer, when he was usually at Schönbrunn, the day's work began at four o'clock. He went through every detail of the documents brought him by an aide-de-camp or the head of a department, signing them with deliberation after reading each page with the greatest care.

Later in the morning he interviewed, as occasion demanded, the Prime Minister, or a Cabinet Minister specially summoned, the Prefect of Police, and invariably the superior officers of the Army, the Commander of the Household Troops, and the Chief of the General Staff; for the Emperor was above all things a soldier and attached the utmost importance to the most trifling matters connected with the Army. Finally there were the private audiences given to individuals. These were not frequent, and did not usually last long. The Emperor received those who sought an audience from him with great simplicity, but whatever might be the standing of his visitors, his manner excluded all familiarity. Franz Joseph had the gift of keeping people at a distance without having recourse to haughtiness or pomposity. He had a genial way, but insisted on the scrupulous observance of the strict rules he had personally established. As head of the House of Hapsburg, he controlled his family with an iron hand, and kept the Archdukes strictly under his thumb. He was such a stickler for punctuality that those who had an appointment with him allowed a quarter of an hour's margin, to avoid any risk of being late. Whenever he attended a public ceremony, orders were issued on the previous day for a carriage, with a team of horses similar to those to be used in the actual procession, to make a trial trip over the route, and for the time to be carefully taken.

At Schönbrunn, the spring and autumn residence of the Imperial family, the daily routine was similar. The Emperor never went out except for official ceremonies at which his presence was necessary, to attend Army manoeuvres, to hunt, or to travel in the states of the Monarchy. Sometimes a reception was held at the Hofburg; a banquet was given in honour of a foreign personage, or a ball to the aristocracy of the country. The most rigid ceremonial, in accordance with Spanish etiquette, was observed at these functions, only those who could prove sixteen quarterings being admitted, and in the strictest order of precedence.

In this connection an anecdote was related, with much relish, about a Russian Grand Duke, who, at a court ball at Buda had asked that the wife of the Commander-in-Chief of the Austro-Hungarian Army should be presented to him. On that occasion it had to be explained to the Grand Duke that the lady in question, though belonging to one of the good families, had not been born within the charmed circle, and that, therefore, however exalted her husband might be, she could not be received at court.

Such was the Emperor's existence, a monotonous existence rendered almost intolerable by the weight of the responsibilities resting on his shoulders. He was sole arbiter of the destinies of the Dual Monarchy. Unaided, he had to solve the intricate problems of ten patchwork states, in which parties and nationalities fought tooth and nail, and the struggles for power were further embittered by racial antipathies. To all these different peoples he was the personification of the unity of the Empire.

A hereditary instinct for kingship, and a profound innate understanding of the political game compensated for his apparent lack of more concrete personal qualities. He performed his harassing task with a skill that amazed the most gifted of his statesmen, for his views were often proved sounder and more far-seeing than their own. But at the end of the day's work he was tired out, and his brain too exhausted to enjoy recreation of any kind. Having never had a spark of imagination, he was thoroughly bored when thrown on his own resources, and found the time lie heavy on his hands in the Hofburg, if unable to go riding in the Prater.

He had made a romantic love-match with a quite young girl, his cousin Elisabeth, daughter of Duke Maximilian of Bavaria. She was a mere child of fifteen when he fell in love with her at first sight. Partly through want of tact, partly through egotism, he failed to keep her love. Her beauty was regal, to use an epithet which, by a rare but not unparalleled coincidence, is entirely applicable. With her superb figure and proud carriage, her noble oval face and large dark eyes, her rather lofty forehead and straight brows, with a suspicion of haughtiness in her look, and the most magnificent hair in the world, at the age of sixteen she seemed the incarnation of the goddess Diana to the enchanted Viennese.

This mere child, a true descendant of the Wittelsbachs, an ardent but melancholy race, lovers of solitude and the arts, soon found that the baubles of a pageant-loving court entirely failed to satisfy the yearnings of her soul. Franz Joseph was quite incapable of understanding her, and soon an ever-widening gap was formed between them. There is no doubt that, as soon as her first passion had subsided, any affinity of soul which may have previously existed, disappeared completely. Still she served him to the utmost of her ability, for she realized what she owed to her rank, although she had come to regret it deeply. After the birth of Rudolph, she felt that she had fulfilled her duty to the Emperor and the Monarchy. From that time she recoiled more and more from appearing at court ceremonies. She pined in the frigid atmosphere of the Hofburg. The empty, vapid amusements, the petty details of the conventions which regulated her every movement, were utterly wearisome to her. She had visions of an untrammelled life of beauty, in which both mind and body would develop, of long rides on horseback in the country and of readings of the Odyssey, of hours of physical culture intermingled with conversations, through books, with great thinkers of the past and of her own day.

Her taste was fearless and original. Almost alone in Germany, she enjoyed the lyricisms and biting verse of Heine. Moreover, she passionately loved nature; the clouds and the sky, the silence of the woods, the murmurs of the earth seemed very far from the Empress caged within the thick walls of the Hofburg, and the slightly over-large ears of the Emperor were better suited for hearing the reports of his functionaries. In Vienna she practised horsemanship in the Spanish riding-school within the precincts of the palace, and her feats were the envy of the best professional horsewomen. She rode the finest animals in the imperial stables, the famous Isabel'ones, which had descended in direct line from the horses of Charles V.

The moment in the year she loved best was the short stay of the court in the castle of Gödöllö, in the heart of the forest of Northern Hungary. There, restraints were almost

entirely relaxed, and she could live close to nature. Her
health, which at times caused anxiety, gave her an excuse
for leaving Austria. Thus she was able to satisfy her passion
for travel by long stays in Madeira, Corfu, the South of
France, England and Normandy.

At the Hofburg there was no escape from the Emperor.
Directly he was free for a moment, between two audiences,
he would arrive. The Empress would hear his footsteps on
the four stairs between their apartments. She was already
beginning to dislike the sound of his long, measured tread.
When he spoke, the mere sound of his monotonous voice,
without an atom of expression or emotion, for he had
schooled himself never to raise its tone, gave her a feeling of
insuperable weariness. But she showed no sign; she let him
discuss the dates for their next move from the capital, tell her
some uninteresting story he had heard in the morning, or
complain of the unceasing worries caused by the administra-
tion of his immense and ramshackle empire. She listened to
him patiently, without the least display of ill-humour; in fact
she always paid the closest attention and gave her advice
when asked. When the Emperor left her she took up again
the book she had laid down, either a poem of Heine or a
novel by Dostoievski, who was just becoming known. It was
sheer delight to her to be carried away from the Hofburg to
a quay in St Petersburg on a white night, or to the market-
town of Stephantchi Kovo with Foma Fomitch; the characters in these books were far more real to her than the gilded
chamberlains, who bowed and scraped in the Hofburg.

The Empress seldom appeared in public. Even in Vienna
she took little part in the Emperor's daily life. As a matter
of fact he wearied her, but she was sorry for him too. She
saw him chained in fetters of his own making to a never-
ending and inconceivably futile task. So, a few years before
the point reached in this story, a singular idea occurred to
her. She proposed to try to find a lady as companion to the
Emperor, who was ageing and needed distraction in his
leisure hours. 'She must be someone in whose society he

could relax and forget the worries of power, someone reliable with a lively and cheerful disposition,' she said to herself. But to discover a suitable person, who would neither intrigue nor serve as the tool of one of the court cliques, was no easy matter.

It seemed a particularly hopeless proposition, in the Viennese court, where life was nothing but ambition and a scramble for place. Of middle-class circles the Empress had no knowledge. There remained the theatrical circles, whose members had always been highly esteemed in Vienna, and mingled freely with society. The Empress recalled an actress of the Burg Theatre who had been presented to her at a charity bazaar. She had recently heard her spoken of in very flattering terms. Madame Schratt was young, comely, and had a cheerful disposition.

The Empress sent for her. Presently she arranged for the Emperor to make her acquaintance, and before long Madame Schratt had won both their hearts by her beauty and unaffected sincerity. The Empress must have been a very good judge of character, for Madame Schratt became the Emperor's close and trusted friend, and remained so for over thirty years, up to the very end. The Emperor saw her every day, either in the Empress's or his own apartments, or else in the flat of a house he purchased for her on the Kärntner Ring, within a stone's throw of the palace. He passed an hour or two there with her every evening.

She often visited the Empress in the morning. There is no doubt that a very genuine friendship existed between the two women. It is, none the less, a most remarkable thing that not once did the Empress have cause to regret the course she had taken. Never did Madame Schratt show any inclination to pry into other people's affairs or to follow the interested advice of those who tried to make use of her influence.

She soon gained the Emperor's confidence so completely that he spoke to her unreservedly on every conceivable subject. She had the knack of taking him out of himself;

she admired his good qualities, she was sorry for him; she was fond of him, too.

Thus, in this ancient palace were forged bonds of amity and mutual esteem between three people of fundamentally different characters. And when the immeasurable greatness of two of them, and the humble origin of the third are considered, and it is remembered what the three had to forget in order to give to the others only the best of themselves, surely a phenomenon presents itself the like of which the world has never seen, will never see again, and which was possible only in the gay and charming atmosphere of Vienna.

Freed from these cares, the Empress freely indulged her craving for solitude and reverie. Had she not sprung from a royal line of princes, unwarlike, averse to action, lovers of the arts, of all that helped them to forget the world, immoderate, moreover, in their passions, indulging them up to that critical point where reason threatens to founder? She was one of them. Like them she longed to escape from herself. She felt ill at ease in the family circle. Her two daughters had very little in common with her. Both were typical Hapsburgs. But Rudolph, charming and chivalrous, wayward and proud, was a true son of his mother. And she often felt sad at the heavy disadvantages she had bequeathed to her gifted son.

An incident, without the least significance, that happened when Rudolph was a very small boy, came back persistently to her mind. The child, in trying to walk, fell heavily to the floor.

'If you can't stand up alone, little man,' she said, laughing, 'how will you ever bear the weight of the double crown?'

His military training began at a tender age. The Emperor considered that habits of discipline could never be learned too young. So the boy grew up under the watchful eye of General de Gondrecourt, an old martinet with narrow and rigid ideas. The Prince was allowed to indulge in neither whims nor fancy. He saw his parents at fixed times and not every day. The Emperor took delight in making him do military drill.

Occasionally the Empress had him entirely to herself. Then she would tell him fairy stories and take him with her into a world of marvels. Both loved to talk of the mysterious existence of elves, dwarfs, and gnomes, who live in the depths of the forests. Such moments, however, were rare and became rarer as time passed by.

Although she loved her son devotedly, the Empress accepted this separation with fatalism. 'All lives are lonely,' she thought, 'and ours more so than those of other people.'

So a barrier grew up between mother and son. She watched him from the distance, wistfully. He was now a man, clever, highly cultivated, with a broad and generous mind, but sensitive, as she was herself, mercurial, highly strung, and impulsive; loving life passionately, yet burning it as a thing of no value.

CHAPTER III

THE LITTLE BLUE FLOWER

LOSCHEK, THE PRINCE'S trusted body-servant since early childhood, entered his master's sleeping apartment at half past seven as usual. He drew the curtains, went into the bathroom, gave some instructions to another servant and put out the Prince's clothes. Then he went over to the narrow bed in the corner of the room. The Prince did not stir. The old valet looked at him fondly for a moment, as he lay there sleeping soundly. Then leaned over and touched him lightly on the shoulder.

An hour later, the Prince began the routine work of the day, in one of the large salons with white and gold wainscoting. An aide-de-camp was waiting for him at a desk on which he had just laid a pile of papers.

The hours passed slowly. There were documents to sign and deputations to receive; there was a council to preside over. The most exhilarating discussion of the morning was with the chief of the ordnance department on the merits of a certain powder used for polishing the buttons of the soldiers' uniforms. This serious matter had to be settled, and the order for it given. The Prince was thoroughly bored, and was not at liberty until noon. He dismissed his aide-de-camp, who reminded him, as he left, that His Majesty was giving a luncheon party in honour of the Prussian princes on their way through Vienna, and said that he would call for the Prince at half-past one.

'Prussian orders must be worn,' he added. 'There are to be races in the Prater in the afternoon.'

As soon as he was alone, the Prince went out by a small door that Loschek unlocked for him. He passed along interminable passages, went up flights of stairs, eventually arriving at a comparatively small room with a low ceiling, and joining the chamber in which he had been sleeping for about a year. It looked on to the Amalien Hof and the windows of the Empress's apartments could be seen from it.

The room had an air of comfort totally unexpected in that austere palace. There were comfortable leather chairs, a sofa with cushions, a Wilton carpet, Persian rugs, vases of flowers, finally a modern desk with a human skull on it. In the middle of the room, hardly recovered from a long and perilous journey through the passages and ante-chambers, stood Herr Szeps.

At the sight of the Prince his face lit up with pleasure. The Prince shook his hand warmly and made him sit down beside him on the sofa. Then he filled two glasses from a decanter that Loschek had just brought in on a salver.

'My dear Szeps,' he began, 'this is my first leisure hour on a horribly dull morning, I place it entirely at your disposal. I will talk as much as you like but, for Heaven's sake, not about business.'

The conversation was quite informal; not one of the Prince's words made his listener feel aware of the difference in their positions. The Prince, who was very much a creature of moods, was obviously in the best of humours and thoroughly at his ease. Political matters were lightly touched on. On hearing the latest news received at the Hofburg, to the effect that the German Emperor Frederick's health was precarious, with a very remote prospect of a permanent cure, Szeps felt a very real dismay.

'If we lost the German Emperor, Sir, disastrous results would follow for the Liberal cause the world over,' he said. 'All lovers of freedom have looked forward with expectation to your Royal Highness ruling in Austria and the Emperor Frederick in Germany simultaneously.'

'That is a thing that my best friends should not wish me, Szeps. But I am afraid that the Germans will soon have my dear cousin William as their master. If he doesn't ruin his dynasty and the country, there must be a special deity who watches over kings and lunatics.'

Szeps raised his arms in despair. He had a vision of the party he had struggled against for years taking a new lease of life, if the progressive German Emperor were lost to them. Like all Jews he excelled in weighing the forces and influences of the unseen. Suddenly, glancing at the heir to the throne at his side, he was struck by the signs of exhaustion in his face, his unnatural pallor, and the dark lines under his eyes. What if they should lose him too? He betrayed the trend of his thoughts by an unexpected question, which was out of place there, or perhaps was too obviously connected with the news he had just heard about the Emperor Frederick.

'Does Your Imperial Highness enjoy good health?'

The question was asked in such a tone of alarm that the Prince burst out laughing.

'Much better than the Emperor Frederick,' he replied, helping himself to another glass of port. 'If I happen to look tired – as a matter of fact I am tired – it is not altogether unnatural. I was up last night until three in the morning with Philip of Coburg. There were fair ladies there, Szeps, and the Tokay was of the best. At half-past seven Loschek showed no mercy and fetched me out of bed as usual. I have had my nose to the grindstone all the morning, without a single breath of fresh air. This afternoon I am going to the races; that will put me into good form again.'

'How anxious Your Highness makes me feel,' said Szeps, leaning towards the Prince.

He had the appearance of an old nurse remonstrating with a child she adores.

Just at that moment the door opened quietly and Loschek came in. Going up to his master he handed him a letter on a silver salver. The Prince recognized the handwriting at once – the note was from the Princess. His mood changed in a flash.

'You know very well, Loschek, that I intensely dislike being disturbed in here,' he said roughly.

'Her Highness commanded that the note should be delivered immediately. I was afraid Her Highness might come in person,' replied the old servant.

The Prince took the letter and begged Szeps to excuse him. After reading it, he threw it on a chair, saying to Loschek: 'There is no answer. Tell Her Highness that I shall be in my apartments at half-past one, on my way to luncheon with the Emperor.'

His voice sounded harsh. The sudden change in his manner astonished Szeps. There was a hard look in the Prince's face, and a flinty gleam in his eyes. He seemed to be making no effort to control his temper; apparently oblivious of Szeps' presence he flew into a violent passion.

'My wife leads me a dog's life,' he raved. 'There's not a corner of the palace I can call my own. She doesn't give me a moment's peace. Devil take her!'

It was the first time he had spoken of the Princess to Szeps in such a tone. Perhaps the hardest part of the life of Royalties is the constant need for dissimulation. There is something appalling in this everlasting obligation to suppress the feelings. It implies the necessity for calculation, even when in a rage. The Prince must have realized intuitively that he could let himself go in front of Szeps on this exceedingly private matter, without risk. The journalist had proved his discretion on previous occasions and his having no connection with the court precluded the possibility of his chattering in court circles. So the Prince allowed himself the luxury of giving full vent to his pent-up feelings.

At this violent exhibition of anger Szeps was completely nonplussed. Outside the realm of ideas he never stood on firm ground. He had not asked for this confidence, and did not know what attitude to adopt. He felt that, when the Prince had recovered his self-control, he would resent his indiscretion, and that their friendship, which he valued greatly, would suffer in consequence. For the moment silence was the only course. He made himself as small as possible and took refuge in a corner of the sofa.

Meanwhile the Prince continued raving about scenes inflicted on him by his jealous wife.

'This will inevitably end in a scandal—'

He strode up and down the room feverishly.

'A scandal!' repeated Szeps, horrified.

'Yes, a scandal. She, at any rate, will do nothing to avoid it. In this letter she again threatens to leave me and return to Brussels.'

'That's impossible, Your Highness,' said Szeps forcibly. 'Absolutely impossible! In your position—'

The last words had an unexpected effect on the Prince. With a gleam of amusement in his eyes, he said: 'Now this is very odd, my dear Szeps; those are the identical words used by the Father Superior of the Jesuits.'

'The Father Superior of the Jesuits!' repeated Szeps, thunderstruck. 'I am afraid that I don't understand.'

'He was here yesterday,' said the Prince, watching with interest the effect of his words on his listener.

Szeps remained dumbfounded. The Prince continued:

'He was speaking of this very matter, at the instigation of the Princess, without doubt. I shall have no more peace if the Jesuits intend to interfere. Before leaving, he hinted that there was no heir to the throne.'

'There, Sir,' interrupted Szeps, 'I think he was right.'

'And in addition,' continued the Prince, 'he put out feelers to ascertain whether any fair usurper of the Princess's place had gained influence over me. I know these people; if there is to be an acknowledged favourite they intend her to be of their choosing.'

Szeps could bear it no longer. He jumped to his feet, exclaiming: 'Take care, I implore Your Highness to be cautious. The Jesuits are the most dangerous people in the world. They work, as they say, *ad majorem Dei gloriam*; for that purpose they are ready to use any means. It would be disastrous, abominable—' He failed to find his words. 'It is impossible!'

This time the Prince laughed out loud. Putting his hand on the journalist's shoulder, he said: 'Don't you worry, my dear Szeps, I am not in their clutches yet.' He stopped talking for a moment. 'But there is a place to be filled – a place to be filled. Think it over, Szeps; it's important.'

There was a pause. The Prince's expression changed again. He walked slowly across the room with bowed head. Suddenly he went over to Szeps, sat down beside him, offered him a glass of port, and, looking him straight in the face, continued in low tones:

'As today we are talking on forbidden subjects, has it ever occurred to you to think about the private life of a man in my position? The poorest devil in the land has the right to choose a wife. *"Il faut que chaque Jeannot trouve sa Jeannette"* wrote Voltaire. But for princes, the State decides. And if I haven't found my Jeannette? *Tant pis.* There is no help for it. You may say that a prince can find ample compensation in other ways. No one knows that better than I. But when one is tied fast to a cantankerous woman, it's not diversion one seeks, but something far harder to find, forgetfulness. Women – it's a curious thing, Szeps, that the subject of women should crop up between you and me, who have never before touched on anything but politics. But with women, you never know! There is nowhere they are not ready to venture.'

He laughed rather wildly, and continued:

'I am the Crown Prince, still young, and unhappily married. Everybody knows that. You may imagine how much that fact arouses, shall we say, feminine curiosity? Yes, they hanker after seeing me at close quarters, and long to try their chance. It provides them with a part to play. Intrigue and love, *Cabale und Liebe*, a programme very attractive to the feminine mind. What woman would not like to try her hand? And why not? Who is not anxious to use influence, or has not an axe to grind? Think, Szeps, of the number of people who have everything to gain by bringing a girl here, into this very room. Think of the proposals with a double meaning, or often frankly cynical, that are made to me. My father is an old man. These people count on my early succession to the throne. They want to take up position in good time, to have a hold upon the Crown Prince. What a priceless opportunity! Who would refuse it?'

The Prince ceased speaking, and his eyes had a distant look, as if he had forgotten the presence of Szeps. His face wore a cynical expression quite foreign to it.

'Who would refuse it?' he repeated, as if to himself. 'Not even you, Szeps, who are the soul of honour. You have a daughter, I believe. If I asked you, would you not bring her to me?'

'But, Your Highness—' cried Szeps in consternation.

'How old is she?' pursued the Prince mercilessly.

'Our Rachel is fifteen,' replied the journalist, losing his head at the unforeseen turn in the conversation.

'Fifteen! That was Juliet's age. It's true that this Romeo is thirty. What does that matter? He may be on the throne tomorrow. That is what counts. That is what must not be forgotten! Then you would have a double hold upon me – with ideas – and in another way too.'

Poor Szeps, in despair at seeing, in such a crude light, the man on whom he had built all his hopes, buried his face in his hands. But the Prince continued cruelly.

'Think of a famous precedent in the history of your own nation. Don't you remember the offering by Mordecai of his niece Esther to King Ahasuerus? What a far-seeing uncle! What a splendid stroke of policy!'

Szeps was very nearly annihilated. At last he plucked up courage to respond:

'Your Highness, Your Highness, I beg you to stop. I cannot let you. I was not expecting— Do not doubt that I have often thought of your lonely life. Having the honour of your friendship, I have often felt distressed about it. How I regret that your exalted station prevents you from frequenting our

circles. Yes, in our circles there are women of noble character, with the finest instincts and highest ideals. You would
find among them a friend on whom you could implicitly
rely for support at the most difficult moments. But our little
Rachel is too young; she is still at school; she is quite un-
developed. For her studies, and because her eyes are weak,
she wears spectacles—'

This was too much for the Prince, who burst out laughing.

'Spectacles! The spectacles have saved little Rachel! Ha,
Ha, Ha!'

His laugh was strained, and affected the overtired nerves
of Szeps. He shrank back on the sofa. What would he not
have given to be back in his *Neues Wiener Tageblatt* office?
How wistfully he remembered the long, impassioned, yet
peaceful discussions with the Crown Prince in that very
room. Here he was on a stormy sea on which he could not
steer his frail barque, expecting another squall to burst. To
keep himself in countenance, he wiped the glasses of his
pince-nez.

The Prince, however, grew calmer. He still strode mechanically up and down the room, but his tense look had disappeared. At last, he sat down in an armchair opposite
Szeps, and addressed him in rather a sad voice, but with the
frankness that gave him such charm.

'I must ask you to forgive me, Szeps. To be perfectly
candid, I am disgusted with the life I lead. Do you think I
was made for debauch? Heaven forbid! I endure it, as a
disease, an incurable disease, alas! For it feeds on disap-
pointed hopes and daily renunciations, on an imperious
longing to forget, on distress at seeing the best and noblest
part of myself slowly vanish beneath a rising flood of bitterness. Deep down in me there is a craving for beauty and
nobility that will not be denied. If I appear cynical, it is
due to an unsatisfied longing for romance deeply rooted in
my heart. There is always there what has been ingenuously
called a little blue flower, a little flower that lives on romance.
It is a hardy little flower, I promise you, Szeps. It protests

and murmurs in its own way. I would gladly stifle its importunate voice, but I cannot. This little flower harbours vain illusions, and whispers of happiness that will never be mine. Bah! I shall smother it yet. I will give you rendezvous here in a year from today.'

He spoke in a tone of irony that did not hide his innate sincerity. Szeps was deeply moved. What a splendid man the Prince was! What a generous and noble nature he had! He felt himself bound to him by ties even stronger than before.

At that moment the door opened gently, and Loschek appeared. The Prince jumped up with a start.

'I was completely forgetting the Emperor's luncheon party. Luckily this old brute,' he said, pointing affectionately at his old servant, 'keeps a strict eye on me. Szeps, don't bear me ill will for the unpleasant hour you have just spent. We will make up for it the next time.'

He hurried off to the salon, where the Princess Stephanie was expecting him at half-past one. Being anxious to avoid the company of the irascible Princess, he had carefully timed his meeting with her in the reception chamber to coincide with the arrival of his aide-de-camp.

CHAPTER IV

12TH APRIL, 1888

WHEN THE IMPERIAL luncheon party was over, the Crown Prince drove with his two Prussian guests in one of the court carriages to the racecourse on the Prater.

All the most distinguished people of Vienna were already on the course. Everyone knew everyone else in that exclusive world. It was exceedingly difficult to get an introduction there, but once the barriers had been raised, the real simplicity and unaffected charm behind them were surprising.

The gay, mercurial, lovable, care-free, at times inconstant Viennese had a peculiar charm. In the operas that have made the Viennese temperament known the world over everything moves to the rhythm of a waltz which caresses the heart, without touching it deeply. In the third act, at the traditional moment when the lovers quarrel, the music, more and still more insistent, sways their passionate disputes, until finally it triumphs, and the lovers fall into each other's arms. It was the haunting music of the waltz, now grave, now gay, that gave life in Vienna its atmosphere and tone.

There are only two cities in the world whose women have understood the art of dressing perfectly, Paris and Vienna. That afternoon Vienna more than justified its reputation for elegance. Beautiful women from every province of the Empire were there, clad, after the fashion of the day, in full gowns with puff sleeves of costly taffetas, silks or velvets, and wearing large picture hats plumed with ostrich feathers or aigrettes. There were laughter-loving Viennese blondes, stately Bohemian aristocrats, almond-eyed Hungarian brunettes, graceful Polish women with mysterious eyes, Servian and Croatian women from the sunny districts of the South.

Courtiers and aristocrats mingled with magnates of finance and famous actors, with that suave urbanity that renders social intercourse so pleasant. Many mothers had brought their daughters, and their bright young faces lent an additional touch of gaiety to the scene.

None of them was more thrilled at the novelty of the experience than a young girl of sixteen, whose first visit it was to a race meeting. She was the daughter of Baroness Vetsera, who came of a rich Levantine family, Baltazzi by name. The Baroness had married one of the Hungarian lesser nobility in the diplomatic service. She had settled in Vienna some years before, and had bought a mansion in the Salezianer Strasse. Being unable to prove the regulation sixteen quarterings, she had not been presented at court, although both the Emperor and the Empress were acquainted with her. She knew all the best people in Vienna, with the possible exception of two or three of the most exclusive families. She had been an extremely pretty woman in her time. With approaching middle-age she became excessively stout, as often happens with women of Eastern origin, but her grey eyes were still remarkable, and she had lost none of the lovableness that had brought her such a host of friends. She was immensely rich, and entertained on a lavish scale. Her four brothers were celebrated sportsmen, and belonged to the best hunting and racing circles in Vienna.

The Baroness had two sons, and two daughters, Hanna and Marie. Hanna was plain; Marie, the younger of them, at the moment when this story begins, was extraordinarily attractive, with the bewitching loveliness of a child. She was tall, slender, and beautifully made, with exquisite little hands and feet; she had masses of black silky hair, and in striking contrast to it, a complexion as fair as a lily. Another feature, quite out of the ordinary, was the contrast between her long dark silky eyelashes and the periwinkle blue of her large eyes. These eyes were sometimes laughing, more often unusually serious for so young a girl. Her nose was rather short, her mouth small and well formed, her teeth of a dazzling whiteness. Lastly, Marie had the most priceless of all gifts, that without which the others count but little, personal charm, divine gift which excites the desire of gods and men.

On leaving the convent where she had been educated, she spent the winter in Egypt with her family. It was only a month since their return to Vienna. While Marie had not yet made her entrance into society, she had already created a distinct sensation in her mother's salon in the mansion in the Saleziner Strasse. She seemed quite unconscious of the interest she aroused and of the compliments that were paid her. Like all the girls of that day, she was strictly brought up and never allowed to go out by herself. In fact, her mother always accompanied her.

The Vetsera ladies met numerous friends at the races. Throughout the afternoon they were overwhelmed with attentions. A young Portuguese, who was connected with the Portuguese royal family, and lived in Vienna, came up to them and chatted with Marie. He offered to put fifty crowns on a horse for her in the second race, which was just about to start.

As they stood talking in the paddock, there was a slight commotion. It was the Crown Prince and the Prussian Princes making their way to their box. Their passage through the paddock caused the usual amount of interest, but was unnoticed by Marie, whose attention was monopolized at the moment by Miguel de Braganza. Her mother and sister were just behind, watching the Princes as they went by. Miguel of Braganza left Marie for a moment, to go into the Ring to place a bet. A movement of the crowd separated her from her mother, and she remained standing alone a few yards away from the centre of the grand stand. On happening to look up, she saw in the imperial box a young man in the uniform of a cavalry general. Something in his bearing and general appearance seemed familiar to her. She stood looking at him for a moment. 'It must be the Crown Prince,' she thought suddenly. He was so much better looking than in his photographs that she did not at first recognize him. Just at that moment the Prince turned his head in her direction, and caught a glimpse of the girl's fresh young face. Struck by her extraordinary beauty, he remained looking at her for a moment. Marie felt ready to sink into the ground; she would gladly have disappeared into the crowd, yet could not free herself from his compelling gaze.

A voice near-by saved the situation:

'Where are you, Baroness, where are you?'

It was Miguel de Braganza on his way back from the Ring. Fortunately he was not at all an observant person, which gave her time to recover her composure. A few minutes later Baroness Vetsera with some friends rejoined her daughter. Marie would have found it very difficult to say how the remainder of the afternoon passed. She followed her mother and sister mechanically, made small talk to acquaintances, and smiled apropos of nothing in particular.

Towards the end of the meeting she summoned up sufficient courage to glance at the Prince's box again. To her great surprise she saw that he was looking in her direction, and seemed to be searching for somebody in the crowd. Then he leaned over toward an officer in the box, and, without removing his eyes, exchanged a few words with him. Next she saw the officer look in the direction of their party before answering the Prince's question.

All that had happened was so obvious that it was impossible to be mistaken about it.

When she got home she retired to her room, and excused herself from dinner on the plea of a headache. She felt overcome with happiness, and wished to be alone.

CHAPTER V

A MAIDEN'S HEART

THE CROWN PRINCE was continually in Marie's thoughts. She saw united in him all the characteristics with which, in books and dreams, she had clothed her beau-ideal of a knight. His character was a blend of opposite qualities. He was both handsome and clever, brave and well-read, chivalrous and circumspect. While perfectly at ease in society, he would go on long hunting expeditions with no companion but a forester. He was fond of wine, music, and the society of women, yet he devoted several hours of every day to arduous duties. Above all things he was a prince, and, after the Emperor, the first gentleman in the land. All these virtues made the stronger appeal because he might have led an idle and dissipated life like so many of the Archdukes.

Marie was thus building for herself an enchanting picture of the Crown Prince. Who could be compared with him? How infinitely superior he was to the men who visited her mother's house! Yet they belonged to the smartest set in Vienna.

To complete her picture, she began to ask her friends questions. Tittle-tattle, at that moment more than ever, was busy with the Prince. His name was on everybody's tongue; hardly a day passed without a new piece of gossip, often entirely untrue, about him. But just as the tender roots of a little tree know how to draw from the soil and absorb only the substances that are nourishing and can aid its growth, so, from everything Marie heard in casual conversations, she selected only what was needed to embellish the portrait of the man who had suddenly become her idol. Slander and everything unpleasant did not appear to reach her ears.

Marie was very skilful with her questions. She put them

cautiously, for she was anxious to keep her secret to herself. Still, what had she to hide? Nothing as yet. She would have laughed if anyone had suggested that she was beginning to fall in love with the Crown Prince. She thought him interesting; he certainly was a splendid man. Just that, and nothing more. But how fascinating it all was! She spent many pleasant hours building castles in the air about him. These feelings seemed to her quite natural; she did not realize that the desire to conceal them was the proof that they were other than she believed.

She kept herself informed of the Prince's movements. The Emperor was always sending him to every quarter of the Empire. One day, it was to Budapest, where he would spend a few days. Hardly back from there – almost before he had been seen in Vienna – he would leave for Prague. His military duties took him to Lemberg or into Bukovina; hunting parties were arranged for him in Bohemia or in the Tyrol. It was impossible to keep count of his travels. Occasionally his movements were kept secret, even from personal friends. Sometimes when it was announced in the press that, after a short absence, His Imperial Highness had returned to Vienna, in fact, he was not there.

Marie's questions were not entirely disinterested. If she was anxious to know if the Prince was in residence at the Hofburg, it was because she hoped for a glimpse of him in the Prater, at the races, or at the theatre. She used every conceivable artifice to find out from her uncles or Miguel de Braganza the most likely moment for meeting him in the Prater! The Baroness Vetsera, who was fond of her home, was astonished at her daughter's becoming a regular little gadabout. She was not content unless she drove in the park every day, and went to the opera at least twice a week. All the same, the Baroness was very proud of her daughter's success and general popularity.

There were times when Marie laughed at herself for the extent to which the Prince absorbed her thoughts. The first thing she read in the morning paper was the court news.

The occasional moving of the court to Budapest was hateful to her, for it necessitated the absence – often for over a week – of the Crown Prince and Princess. The Crown Princess she did not like. She knew, as did everyone in Vienna, that the marriage was an unhappy one. Who was to blame? It was, of course, the fault of Stephanie, the big, stupid, clumsy Belgian woman. Marie was quite at a loss about the matter. The Princess had the wonderful good fortune to be married to the most attractive man in the Empire, yet she was unable to make him happy. Sometimes Marie used to imagine herself for a moment in a similar position. What loving care she would have lavished on a man like that! At night, when she indulged in dreams of her idol, she was unable to sleep. Rudolph (she always thought of him by his Christian name) was near her; she was talking to him; she could feel the magic of his touch.

One night at the opera, while Marie and her mother were chatting with friends in the lobby of the dress circle, the Prince and Princess came right upon them. There was just room to allow the Royal pair to pass. As they moved by, the Prince was so close as almost to touch Marie. He was answering a question of the Princess at the moment, and, his back being turned to Marie, he obviously did not see her. Had he noticed her before? She asked herself this question later. At the moment she was surprised to find a tight feeling in her heart at the unexpected sight of the Royal couple. She had often heard Rudolph spoken of as a married man, but until that night had never seen him with his wife. Seeing them together was the transformation of a vague idea into reality. It was a new experience for her – and a distressing one.

On that occasion, although her idol was in the theatre, she spent a miserable evening.

For a time Marie had been quite content to think of the Crown Prince and to endue him with all the virtues. But soon she wondered what impression she had made on him. She was quite convinced he had noticed her; perhaps he had admired her – at the races and elsewhere. But before long doubts began to arise. 'He certainly looked at me,' she said to herself, 'but it may, of course, have been because he saw me for the first time. He knows everyone in Vienna, and I was unknown to him. If he noticed me, it was not out of admiration, but curiosity. I am so young. Why should he be interested in me?'

At other moments, she decided he had found her attractive. 'Surely I must be pretty and attractive,' she thought, 'as all the men I meet are always telling me so. But, alas! in the Empire there are more beautiful women than I who are lucky enough to know him. He sees them every day of his life. He is *blasé*, I am sure he has forgotten me already. The first time I meet him he won't recognize me.'

She was beginning to feel miserable, but she did not know that it is on such doubts and anxieties that a growing love feeds, and that bonds were gradually forming, the power of which was destined to surprise her soon.

A month passed thus. The Prince was travelling; or, if he was in Vienna, she caught no glimpse of him. At last, early in May, a gala night at the Burg Theatre was announced in honour of the greatest German tragedian of the day. All Vienna would be there, and the Crown Prince was to honour the performance with his presence. Marie urged her mother to take tickets without delay. The play was to be *Hamlet*.

'It's a tedious and depressing play,' objected the Baroness Vetsera to her daughter. 'Are you quite sure you want to go? I should be frightfully bored.'

But Marie usually managed to get her way, and the Vetseras booked a box.

On the evening of the play, Marie spent longer than usual over her toilet. After very careful consideration, she decided upon a simple white muslin dress, in which she looked charming. The box she had chosen was quite close to the Imperial box. The Crown Prince and Princess made their entry a little late, when the theatre was almost in darkness, during the scene in which Hamlet invokes his father's ghost on the terrace of Elsinore.

At the beginning of the first interval people kept moving in and out of the Imperial box. Marie contrived to watch this without attracting attention. All of a sudden the Crown Prince, who was standing with his back to her, turned round, and, as if previously aware of her presence, fixed his eyes directly upon her. His look seemed to convey both admiration and the pleasure of meeting a kindred spirit again. Yes, his look was eloquent of both these things; and, to prevent any doubt about his meaning, the shadow of a smile accompanied his glance.

Marie was quite overcome. She blushed to the roots of her hair, and, placing her handkerchief to her face, as if to prevent a coughing fit, she sought refuge in the little room behind their box. There, while inwardly delighted, she reproached herself bitterly. 'He recognized me,' she said to herself. 'He hasn't forgotten me! But he must take me for a blushing schoolgirl.'

Later in the evening her courage returned. Circumstances, however, were less propitious. The Prince spent a considerable time away from the Imperial box, Marie was busily engaged with her numerous friends and admirers. In the scene between Hamlet and Ophelia, she was deeply moved at Ophelia's sufferings and hopeless love. But soon her pity was concentrated on Hamlet. The actor playing that part was not unlike the Crown Prince, and she seemed to see him in the guise of the Prince of Denmark.

During the last interval her eyes and the Prince's met again. This time her expression betrayed her love, although she was quite unconscious of the fact.

She lived for days on the memory of that evening. The fleeting smile on the Prince's face opened the gates of Paradise for her. It had conveyed a more subtle and tender meaning than could be expressed by words. Such joy seemed almost beyond belief. She felt blissfully happy.

Then a spell of bad weather set in. The Baroness refused to go driving in the Park. Several days went by without her seeing the Prince. She was beginning to get fretful, when, to her great joy, she saw him twice in the same day in the Prater. He was on horseback; she was driving with her mother and sister. He passed by them quite slowly. Although Madame Vetsera knew both the Emperor and Empress, she had never been presented to the Crown Prince. So he passed without acknowledging them, but he gave Marie the same look of tender admiration as on the night at the opera. Again she became confused, and blushed furiously. Her embarrassment increased at the thought that her mother would notice it and question her. Fortunately, Madame Vetsera had observed nothing.

While driving back by the main avenue the ladies met the Prince a second time. Once more he looked at Marie, who had only just recovered her self-possession; she blushed again. Was it by design that he returned that way? She could not help thinking that it was so.

The next day the same thing happened. Marie was radiant. Her mother and sister spoke in flattering terms of the Prince. Without causing remark, she could add her word to their eulogies.

When she got home she questioned herself searchingly. Could there be any doubt that the Prince had found pleasure in seeing her? But why did she blush whenever he looked at her? What must he think of her? It was true that she admired him. Was that a reason for her losing control of herself? After all, she didn't care for him. At least, so she thought. A definite event was needed to enlighten her.

The Baroness Vetsera had long planned to take her daughters to England for the summer. The matter had often been discussed in the boudoir in the Salezianer Strasse. Now the time was drawing near. Madame Vetsera, who had a great many friends in London, proposed to arrive there about the middle of June, in time for the season. Later they would pay a round of visits in the country. It was already late in May, and necessary to fix a definite date for their departure.

So, what had hitherto appeared to Marie merely a vague proposal became a matter with which she had to reckon. She felt she simply could not leave Vienna. Vienna, to her, she saw it plainly now, was the Crown Prince; it was he, and he alone, that made life worth living. She passed her days in thinking of him, in recalling the minutest details of the last time she had seen him, and in looking forward with delight to their next meeting. The distress she felt at the thought of leaving Vienna was a clear proof to her of the extent to which the Prince filled her heart.

When she made this discovery, she was not distressed. Yet she knew the man she loved only by sight, and the barriers between them seemed insuperable. Even had they not existed, what could she hope for from a man who was heir to the throne and already married? Nothing but heartburnings and vain hopes. Indeed, so rigid was court etiquette in Vienna, that the prospects of her even being presented to the Crown Prince were remote. This child of sixteen was perfectly aware of all these things.

Yet she would see only one thing; that she loved the noblest and best man in the world. Her sole joy – there was none to be compared with it – was to meet him two or three times a month, to admire him from a distance, and to feel his eyes resting on her. That was all she asked. Why should she be deprived of this innocent pleasure? No, she would not go to England. She begged her mother to give up the idea, but Madame Vetsera could see no reason for changing her plans to satisfy a mere whim of her daughter. Marie was in despair; she was afraid, too, that directly he lost sight of her, the Prince would forget about her existence. The bond between them was so unsubstantial. It would snap, if she disappeared. She thought that the only chance of staying in Vienna would be to fall ill. She decided to eat nothing. That she found easy, as her troubles had taken away her appetite. The effect of this on her child's health merely decided Madame Vetsera to hasten their departure. Evidently Marie needed a change of air.

There was only one person in whom Marie confided – her faithful old nurse, a Hungarian peasant-woman, who had looked after her from babyhood. From the very first, she uttered no word about her feelings to either her mother or her sister Hanna. She chatted about it freely to her old nurse who, knowing her young mistress to be purity itself, saw no harm in it. Marie would say, for instance: 'You know, I've just seen the Crown Prince; he is far more handsome than in his portraits.' A little later on, brimming over with happiness, she would say: 'He looked at me in the Prater today. He rode up and down the Avenue twice; I'm sure it was to see me again.'

The old nurse, with her trustful knowledge of the child's innocence, was perfectly content to see her happy. On another occasion, matters went a little further. 'Today, Nannie, he looked at me, as if he were fond of me.' Her nurse, in whose eyes Marie was still a child, again smiled at these girlish whims. She was in no way disturbed, until Marie became upset, in June, at the thought of leaving Vienna. The old woman's uneasiness then was not altogether surprising, as Marie, in her distress, opened her whole heart to her.

'I love him, Nannie, I love him, and never will I love any man but him.'

At this she opened her old eyes wide. Taking Marie's feverish hand, she said: 'You must be crazy, my little lovey. A little girl like you mustn't fall in love with the Crown Prince. Such people are far above us. They don't even know us. What do you expect from him?'

'I expect nothing,' replied Marie. 'I love him, and that's an end of it. I'm perfectly content to see him from a distance, and to know he is looking at me. I want nothing more. Surely they will leave me at least that.'

The old nurse sighed and said nothing more. It was of no use opposing Marie in her present state of excitement. The trip to England and the distractions of the journey would make her forget all about the Prince. On her return she would be the first to laugh at her former fancies.

A few days later the Vetsera family left Vienna.

PART II

CHAPTER I

A DECISIVE STAGE

BY SEPTEMBER the Vetseras were back in Vienna. In England, where Marie had made a great impression, she had not been in such good spirits as usual. Her mother often found her silent, and asked her about it, but she was very far from guessing the cause of the depression.

'Some day,' Madame Vetsera used to say, 'my daughter will come and tell me that she is engaged to be married. That is the way with young people nowadays.'

Marie was then in the first bloom of her loveliness. She was at that delightful time of life when the charms of two ages merge. The pensiveness of the child is still there, showing itself in an expression or a movement of hesitation, but signs of approaching maturity herald the coming triumph of the woman. And her secret deepened the mystery of her eyes, and lent her smile a new charm.

When compliments were paid her she did not hide her pleasure. 'I am all the more sure to please him,' she thought.

During her absence in London, the picture of the Crown Prince in her mind did not grow less vivid. On the contrary, viewed from a distance, he seemed, like mountain peaks, more imposing. He dominated her thoughts so completely that she compared every man she met with him. She felt irresistibly drawn toward him. Had she not already suffered at his hands, wept and blushed with joy and confusion because of him? When she saw her old nurse again, and could at last talk about the Prince, she said to her: 'I love him even more than in the Spring.' The feeling with which she said these simple words was not lost on the old woman, but she merely raised her eyebrows and made no answer.

The Crown Prince was taking part in the Army manoeuvres when Marie arrived in Vienna. Her only compensation during the next fortnight was the melancholy
satisfaction of following his movements in the newspapers.
She regretted not having returned in August; he was at
Laxenbourg then, and in the capital nearly every day.

Moreover, out-of-season life was very tedious in Vienna.
Most society people were still in the country enjoying the
hunting season. The only diversion for the Baroness and
her daughters was the daily drive in the Prater. But its deserted avenues seemed utterly forsaken to Marie without the
Prince's presence. He was never absent from her mind. She
felt sure that he had forgotten her. It was over two months
since he had seen her. She felt that, in less time than that,
she must have passed out of his mind entirely.

It was then that Marie first met a woman who, she little
suspected, was to play so tragic a rôle in her life. One morning Madame Vetsera, who had been out shopping alone,
brought back a friend to luncheon. She was Countess
Larisch, a very pretty and stylish woman of nearly forty.
She had not seen Marie since she had left the convent, and
was greatly struck by her beauty. Marie was even more impressed by her. The fact was that Countess Larisch, being
the daughter of Duke Louis of Bavaria, the elder brother of
the Empress, and of an actress whom he had morganatically
married, was the Crown Prince's first cousin. As a girl, she
had been a favourite of the Empress and had lived a good
deal with the Imperial family. Of late years, for more or less
mysterious reasons, the Empress had ceased to take notice of
her. The fact, however, remained that she was the Prince's
cousin; and she evidently knew every detail of his private
life, and could see him when and where she wished. Marie
welcomed her with rapturous feelings.

During luncheon there was a good deal of talk about the
Prince, who had just returned to Vienna. According to the
Countess, who had a very uncharitable disposition, his matri-
monial relations were going from bad to worse. But while

she said every conceivable unkind thing about the Princess, she uttered not a word against her cousin. Not being in the good books of either the Emperor or the Empress, her only hope of keeping in touch with the Imperial family was Rudolph. She therefore refrained from venting her natural malevolence at his expense. While she exercised her ill-will freely on the Emperor, the Empress and Madame Schratt, she said many nice things about Rudolph. This was in no way a deliberate design for the purpose of impressing Marie, but was perhaps fatal to her. If she had heard her hero belittled or vilified, she would undoubtedly have mistrusted the Countess. As it was, Marie found her the most charming and loyal of women, and was ready to pour out her pent-up feelings to her newly found friend.

As chance would have it, after luncheon, the Countess and Marie were left alone together for a time. It was too good an opportunity to miss. Marie promptly took advantage of it to talk about the Prince. She did so with such warmth that the Countess, with over twenty years of court life to her credit, was not long in guessing the girl's secret. A few sympathetic questions and a display of kindly interest soon showed her exactly how the ground lay. Marie's personal charm at that time was irresistible, and there is no doubt that the Countess came under its influence. But her ingrained love of intrigue decided her to take the earliest opportunity of telling her cousin of the love he had stirred up in the heart of the prettiest girl in Vienna. *Blasé* as he was, the girl's rare and virginal beauty would, she believed, attract him.

Meanwhile, after the Countess had left, Marie could hardly contain her joy. With the aid of her friend she would always know about the Prince's movements and plans in good time. That, in itself, was immensely comforting....

Quick as lightning her thoughts flashed a stage further. Perhaps, one day she would be able to exchange a message with him! The very idea left her breathless. She saw the abyss between herself and the Prince suddenly bridged. He had left a distant planet and come down to earth. He was now very near. Countess Larisch could perhaps bring him even closer. She, Marie, might speak to him! ... All this savoured of the miraculous. Marie was far away in her enchanting dream, and entirely oblivious of her mother and sister chatting beside her. Her thoughts carried her a stage further. Suddenly she shuddered....

The Crown Prince was at Prague, occupied with the eternal round of councils, audiences, receptions and ceremonies, and, in spare time, with shooting or hunting. Every evening it was his lot to sup with pretty women and to drink far into the night. It was a life such as has been led in different countries by other heirs to a throne. They were stigmatized as debauchees by public opinion of the day, but none the less often proved great kings. At times the Prince seemed to accommodate himself to this life perfectly. He could hold his own with the deepest drinkers; and in affairs of the heart he was no less successful. He seemed to be impervious to fatigue. However late he might be at night, he was ready to begin the official day's work the first thing in the morning.

But at other times he loathed himself for the misuse of his gifts and his wasted opportunities. He felt he was destroying the finest and best part of himself. One day, in a discussion with a friend, he took the view that suicide, as practised by the ancients, was both noble and justifiable. 'Why should we fear it?' he said. 'After all, my life is nothing but a succession of suicides.' He was gradually realizing, too, that the lofty political ideas of his youth were in vain. Instead of finding scope for them, he had to wrestle daily about trivial matters with politicians who were either hidebound or corrupt. He found himself unable to cope with the wear and tear of the struggle. What was he to do? Escape? Drink, which is also flight?

Life at home with its everlasting disputes with his sour-tempered wife sickened him. Nor did his short-lived love affairs bring any consolation to his saddened heart. But what was most terrible of all was the feeling of being caught in a trap, with each successive hour of the day fixed long in advance by an irresistible power, in accordance with a programme as immutable as the solar system. Some days he gave way to evil forebodings that preyed upon his mind. 'The ancestral spirits are returning,' he would say gloomily: 'I cannot send them to hell; it is they that will take me there.' The only effective remedy, at such moments, was solitude in the presence of nature. The sanest part of his complex personality found renewed vigour directly he left the feverish haunts of mankind for the quiet of the country.

Before leaving Prague, he arranged for a short shooting expedition on an island in the Upper Danube. He started alone. He desired no companion but the foresters. For two days he lived in a shelter in the forest. Here was the peace for which he craved. No spies, no police guarding him, no mail to answer, no indiscreet women to beguile him. In the place of importunate friends and the cares of State, there were wild flowers, woods, and running water; higher up, the mountains and the virgin snow, higher still, the sky and the clouds.

Here he was in harmony with the mysterious powers of nature; here he could see the aspen leaf quiver at sunset, and the grass blades unbend at dawn, and could feel the shy welcome of the harebell nestling in the mossy turf. What were the camelias and azaleas in his mother's drawing-room in comparison with this delicate dew-kissed little flower? He felt the mute appeal that rises from the depths of the forest at noon, when the sullen heat weighs down the flagging vegetation. Sometimes, when stalking a deer, he lay motionless along the bough of a tree. Here, with the contact of his body against the fresh bark, he forgot the deer he was expecting, the free lord of the forest like himself, he forgot his own existence, became one with the tree, his brother, which he embraced, feeling its sap rising within him.

*   *   *

By October, Vienna had filled up. The court was at the Hofburg; the Imperial theatres were opening; from a hundred taverns floated the strains of waltz music, while people, on their way home from the theatre, sipped Pilsener or white Weidlinger; the Café Sacher had begun to welcome its aristocratic clientèle. It was the most famous of the gay restaurants in Vienna, and had private rooms, to which the Archdukes and the Crown Prince himself often came to finish the evening.

The Prince was soon in harness, and, as usual, engaged up to the hilt with his duties and pleasures. So close did the one follow upon the other that they seemed to form an endless chain, from which there was no escape.

He accepted, without complaint, his military duties and the drudgery of ceremonials entailed by his exalted station; such things were more or less necessary, and served a purpose. But he felt unable to breathe in the stormy atmosphere of his home. His wife either raged or sulked for days on end; and her ceaseless warfare against him became more and more unbearable.

That autumn an incident exasperated him more than usual. One evening he had gone to see a famous Polish Society beauty, Countess Czewucka. For such expeditions he always hired a landau driven by one Bratfisch, a well-known Viennese character. Bratfisch was absolutely discreet and devoted to him. This Bratfisch, a cheery fellow, had earned quite a reputation by his art of whistling, and was often engaged to whistle after supper parties at Sacher's. On the night in question he was waiting with his landau outside Countess Czewucka's house in the Waaggasse. The Princess was at the theatre, and the nearest way back to the Hofburg was by the Waaggasse. After the theatre she drove back home that way, and spied Bratfisch and his carriage waiting at the Countess's door. Too many people of the Court were interested in embroiling the Imperial couple for her not to be cognizant of her husband's flirtation with the pretty Polish woman. She was also perfectly aware that the Prince often employed Bratfisch. Her husband, moreover, when declining to accompany her to the theatre, had given a very lame excuse. Putting two and two together, she jumped to the conclusion that the Prince was behind the closed shutters in the Countess's house.

Without a moment's hesitation, she stopped her carriage, got out, and ordered Bratfisch to drive her back to the Hofburg. This placed the unfortunate fellow in a decidedly awkward position. He could hardly refuse to carry out an order of Her Imperial Highness. He realized, too, that a refusal might result in an even greater scandal, the Princess being quite capable of ringing the bell of the Countess's house. In a flash, he summed up the situation, and making the best of a bad business replied:

'As Your Imperial Highness wishes.'

So, after instructing her own landau, with its coachman and footman in the Imperial livery, to wait outside the Countess's door, the Princess drove off in Bratfisch's carriage. The comments of the servants after seeing her arrive in it at the Hofburg may be imagined.

Within twenty-four hours the latest scandal was known by everyone at the court, and very soon came to the ears of the Emperor, who was furious at the Princess's action. The motto of those who are placed by their exalted position in the public view is, in the words of the Evangelist: 'Woe to that man by whom the scandal cometh.'

The Prince had always exercised the greatest care in observing this rule of the code. But the conduct of a Princess who gave publicity to matrimonial dissensions was entirely reprehensible. There were no two opinions on that matter.

The story was not long confined to court circles. It was soon hinted all over Vienna. The cleavage between the Imperial couple was now public property, and caused considerable perturbation in certain circles, where stress was laid on the Prince having the support of a tactful and entirely dependable wife. The question was discussed in all its aspects in the private office of the *Neues Wiener Tageblatt*, among other places.

Shortly afterward there was a grand ball at Tegernsee. It was a particularly brilliant affair, the entire Viennese aristocracy, the Prince and the Princess, being present. He met his cousin, Countess Larisch, there for the first time since his return to Vienna. While he had no particular liking for her, they were on friendly terms. She always showed him both affection and devotion, and there was always the consideration that some day she might be useful. The policy in courts is the same for high and low: to hurt nobody's feelings and to prepare supporters in case of need. Just as in a building, a time of strain may come when a single bolt is as necessary as a main girder.

That evening the Prince was in an excellent humour. The wines and especially the champagne, had been to his liking; the women were good to look at; the atmosphere was genial. Countess Larisch, who had a special reason for wishing to see him, eventually contrived to get a *tête-à-tête*.

'My dear Rudolph,' she began, 'what an enviable position you have. Not content with being the hope of the Monarchy, you have played Don Juan so successfully, that you show signs of being *blasé*. Still, if it will amuse you, I will tell you of a conquest you have made without your ever suspecting it.'

The Prince had listened a hundred times to similar stories, which had usually ended with a sufficiently brutal offer. Nor would he have been greatly surprised, had his cousin, who was a born intriguer, attempted to influence him for some purpose of her own.

'What are you driving at, Marie?' he asked rather curtly.

'My dear Rudolph,' she replied, 'what I have to tell you is the most harmless thing in the world. It's just a delightful fairy story. You find that quite interesting, eh? A young and exceedingly pretty girl has fallen madly in love with you, merely on seeing you. That's flattering now, is it not? Had it been your aide-de-camp, it would have been just the same, for this time it's a question of love, genuine love, a Juliet—'

'And what is the young lady's name?'

The Countess was not disposed to tell him at once.

'She is in society, my dear boy. It would be very indiscreet.'

'Come, Marie, you are dying to tell me, and it's the very thing you have come to see me about,' interrupted the Prince good-humouredly.

'You are just as tyrannical as ever,' retorted the Countess. 'You always get your way in the end. The girl is Baroness Marie Vetsera.'

The Prince made an involuntary movement. Marie Vetsera. That name was associated in his mind with a charming vision of fresh and unsullied beauty, with the unknown, and with glances in an avenue of the Prater or at the theatre, in a mute complicity of a few seconds.

'She's perfectly charming!' he declared.

'I told you she was pretty.'

'Pretty! She is far more; she is perfectly charming,' repeated the Prince with enthusiasm. 'She is infinitely more beautiful and has a far more attractive personality than any other girl in Vienna. I have only seen her two or three times from a distance, but I have not forgotten her. Please tell her so from me.'

'She will be wild with joy,' the Countess assured him. 'She is still a child. How proud she will be to think you have noticed her!'

The Prince left his cousin and went over to a group, in the midst of which sat the beautiful Polish Countess who had captured his attention for a while.

CHAPTER II

EDDIES

THROW A STONE into a raging sea, it disappears without leaving a trace. Throw one into a calm mill pond, it sets up a movement in the waters. At the point of contact, ever-widening circles are formed, which expand to the edge of the pond. The entire surface of the water is affected by the vibration.

The calculated indiscretion of Countess Larisch fell upon a man who was just like a sea lashed by the winds. For him there was no peace; his life was a ceaseless torment, under the constant pressure of a thousand distracting influences. Yet the name of Marie Vetsera made an impression upon him.

The Prince found it soothing to recall her sweet pure face. She was still a child, and she loved him! More than once his thoughts dwelt upon her. But she was a charming girl with a host of admirers; her fanciful love for him would soon pass. Yet she did not seem to be a coquette. There had appeared a sedateness behind her eyes, when sometimes they had met his own. He wished to meet her again, but his life took him this way and then that. When would he see her again? Probably she would fall in love with another and be married.

Meanwhile, when Countess Larisch next saw Marie, and she was not long in finding an opportunity, she reported the Prince's words. Marie blushed – she could not yet keep back her blushes when she heard Rudolph's name – but said nothing. She merely took the Countess's hands in hers. Her mother was just entering the room.

During the remainder of the visit, Marie remained silent. As the Countess was leaving, she said to her aside: 'Come back as soon as you can, I have something to say to you.'

During the few minutes spent there by the Countess, Marie had taken at a leap the walls that had hitherto bounded her horizon. At first, it had satisfied her to see the Prince. The happiness she drew from that filled the entire day. But since the night at the opera, when he had looked at her so tenderly, she was not happy unless she had exchanged looks with the man she loved. How infinitely remote he was from her!

The arrival of Countess Larisch on the scene had suddenly brought him within reach. Marie could talk about him with someone who had known him since childhood, belonged to his family, had easy access to him, and knew a thousand interesting things about him. She had scarcely begun to revel in this unexpected happiness, to consider it in all its aspects and to become accustomed to the idea of it, when she realized its limitations and felt their terrible restraint. Then, all of a sudden, the stifling prison walls fell down as if by magic, opening up before her new and enchanting vistas.

It seemed as if, through some good fairy, her fondest hopes had been realized. She had longed to exchange messages with the Prince. Lo and behold! the very words he had used about her, reached her. He found her charming – was not that better than either pretty or beautiful? Charming – so she pleased him, he did not confine himself to admiration. And he wished her to know! Marie was spellbound with joy; she dared not build castles in the air, or even look into the future.

Suddenly an alarming thought occurred to her. The Countess had told her the Prince's words; but what had she said in speaking of her, Marie, to the Prince? Did he know that she loved him? Without any doubt, the Countess must have told him this very private secret. At first her modesty, her pride, and all her maidenly feelings revolted. When she was alone in her room she felt ashamed, and tears came to her eyes. The old nurse was alarmed, and asked:

'What is it, my darling?'

'I don't know,' replied Marie, bursting into tears and flinging herself into the old woman's arms. 'I don't know – I'm so happy!'

Several days passed, Marie became impatient again. The god of love is an exacting deity; a compact with him is not possible. He is crafty, too; he asks for only one thing, but, if it be given, he must have more immediately. In truth, he is not content until he has secured all. What had lately made Marie supremely happy now appeared hardly worth having.

After her last meeting with the Countess, it seemed an age before she saw the Prince again in the Prater. With what impatience she had looked forward to the next meeting! What felicity she expected from it! Alas! Her joy was only partly realized. She was only able to glance at him hurriedly, for, as he passed, her mother was speaking to her. She felt so miserable that she could hardly keep back her tears. Her lot was too cruel! When she recovered, chagrin gave place to anxiety. He must have found her cold and indifferent. Or perhaps he would take her for a coquette, who turned away, as soon as she knew she pleased him. Both alternatives were equally unbearable. She longed to justify herself. If only the Countess Larisch had been available, she would have explained what had happened. She would have told Rudolph that Marie – Ah! what could she say to him?

Three days later she was at the opera. The Prince was there too. This time she could look at him at her leisure. He even gave her the suspicion of a smile. But her delight was short-lived, for she saw he looked unwell. Yes, he had grown thin and pale, and his eyes looked hollow and feverish. She was frightened. Either he was already ill, or an illness was impending. Naturally the people round him saw nothing. Who watched him as she, Marie, did? They would not notice until too late. How dreadful it was to be there, so near him, and not to be able to fly to his help! She knew he was leaving the next day for Galicia, a long and fatiguing journey. He would fall ill on the way, far from her. Marie felt wretched.

That night she had no sleep. During the next few days she astonished the footman by sending for the newspapers the first thing in the morning. She scoured them greedily for news of the heir to the throne. Not a word about his precious health could she find.

Thus Marie's days passed. She lived in a state of feverish expectation – Of what?

CHAPTER III

POLITICS

MARIE HAD NOT been alarmed at the opera without reason. She had attributed to a moral crisis the signs of exhaustion her keen eyes had read in the Prince's face. It would not have surprised her to find that she herself played no part in it. He filled the whole of her life, but she had no illusion about the tiny place she held in the thoughts of the heir to the throne of the Hapsburgs. She wondered whether he had thought of her, even once, since he had last seen her?

The Crown Prince was the centre of a thousand intrigues. Crafty schemers fought assiduously round him to ingratiate themselves for their own base ends. He took a profound and genuine interest in politics. He was not a sceptic, who saw in them nothing but a mere game of cards played on a larger scale and with greater cunning. Generous and liberal by nature, he desired more justice, more freedom, and greater well-being for his people. He loathed despotic methods and the maxim beloved by those in power: *Divide et impera*. Their lack of feeling and human sympathy was utterly repugnant to him. He was surrounded by men whose ideas he detested. He had to receive them courteously and amiably. Being naturally impulsive, he had needed a long and arduous schooling to give him the prudence indispensable for his position.

He craved for friendship, but where could he turn for a friend? Those who approached him, however disinterested they might appear, were self-seekers hoping to make use of him. For Philip of Coburg and Count Hoyos he had the feelings one has for boon companions or fellow-sportsmen. They asked for nothing; neither did they give very much. But the rest! Was there a single one who came into his

presence without a lively expectation of favours to come?
No, even his friends of the Liberal press, who speculated for
the distant future, but for a vast stake, had their axes to
grind. Even, perhaps above all, the women he liked and
fondly believed were of his own choosing, had probably
been set on his track for some special purpose. There was not
a soul he could rely on. It was a bitter thought. It preyed on
his mind and was knocking him to pieces.

Nor was there one of his family to whom he could speak
freely. He never mentioned politics to the Emperor. Their
opinions were as wide apart as the poles; any conversations
between them on that subject had been entirely formal. He
felt instinctively that the Empress had tender feelings for
him, though her reticence and reserve became more marked
as time went on. Her liking for solitude and travel was increasing; she had entirely ceased from attending official
ceremonies; no one, not even her son, was admitted into her
confidence. Sometimes from a word of playful banter, from
a look of love or even of pity, he guessed that she still kept a
loving place for him in her heart. But if he gave any sign of
suspecting it, or made any overture, she withdrew into herself at once.

He was on intimate terms with only one of his relatives,
Archduke John Salvator of Tuscany. Although the Archduke was his senior by six years, they had been playfellows.
John was devoted to the Army, and a fine soldier, but the
Prince was attracted to his cousin for quite other reasons.
He was the only member of the Imperial family with liberal
ideas. Moreover, he put his theories into practice, and was
endeavouring to arrange for himself the life of an ordinary
individual. He had fallen in love with a delightful girl of the
Viennese middle classes, Milli Stubel by name. They were
deeply attached and lived very happily together. Usually,
they spent the evening at Milli's sister's house, without any
formalities. The Prince had a great admiration for his
cousin, who, in his opinion, had chosen the better part. He
envied him for having been able to make for himself a

happy family life, with a girl who loved him, so near the redoubtable Hofburg with its shams and starched ceremonials. How tempting it was, but such joys were not for him!

One evening he was discussing the subject with his cousin. Milli Stubel was there, busy with some work near them.

'To tell you the truth,' said John Salvator, 'I'm beginning to get a little tired of life in this country. The delights of pomp and circumstance soon pall. Milli, my dear, come here,' he said, turning round to the girl.

She came, threw her arms round his neck, and kissed him.

'Milli is everything to me,' he continued. 'I expect you agree with me that taking meals with her here is considerably more pleasant than attending family parties or State dinners at the Hofburg. Here we can talk freely without being bored to death by Uncle Albrecht's pompous absurdities.' Archduke Albrecht, the victor of Custozza, was John Salvator's pet aversion. 'Milli doesn't look upon me as an Archduke, but as the man she loves, a very different thing. My only regret is that I am still an Imperial Highness in this country. What I crave for is liberty. One of these days I shall clear out of the country. It wouldn't break my heart to give up my titles and precious privileges. And this little girl would be just as happy as I should. I should leave Austria. There's plenty of room in the world, Rudolph. I love the sea. I can hear the South Seas calling. We would take our time over it, and go in a sailing vessel.'

'You would have to come with us,' said Milli to the Prince. 'You could be the admiral, if you liked, and command the ship.'

'I should have to take a nice little girl, as good as gold, like you,' he replied. 'My cousin John is a lucky fellow.'

Afterwards, he thought of this conversation. To start life over again! Who longed to start life over again more than he did? But one does not start alone on a new life. Whom would he take with him? He could think of no one for the moment, and he felt poor indeed. Then a vision of Marie

Vetsera's sweet young face passed across his mind. There
was something impassioned and serious in her eyes that was
unforgettable. Perhaps she would be ready to give up everything, without asking anything in return. ... He shrugged
his shoulders. 'I shall always be an incorrigible dreamer,' he
thought.

*   *   *

What kept Archduke John Salvator in Austria was ambition. He was a man with ideas; he wished to fight for them
and see them triumph. He looked forward eagerly to playing a part in a new and progressive Empire under the rule of
his cousin Rudolph. All his hopes were centred on him.
Meanwhile he followed the bent of his hasty impulsive
nature. He openly criticized the theories of the Commander-
in-Chief and of the General Staff. He even wrote articles and
pamphlets on military matters both in Austria and abroad.
Such things the Hofburg would never forgive. Recently the
Emperor had forbidden the Crown Prince to see Archduke
John. The order had annoyed him intensely; still he had
had to obey. Gradually, however, in spite of the Emperor's
veto, he secretly renewed contact with his cousin.

John Salvator was getting impatient. The Emperor was
nearly sixty, and seemed as robust as ever.

'Your father works like a machine,' he used to say to
Rudolph. 'Having no feelings, he gives out nothing, so he
doesn't wear out. He may last a long time.'

'Do you mean to stand this for ever?' he ventured one day.

Rudolph gave no reply.

While John Salvator's advanced opinions cost him the
enmity of official circles, he gained the sympathy of the
Liberals and had a following in the Navy. He became tacitly
recognized as a leader, but, as such he was obliged to work
with the utmost caution. Activities which have to be carried
on in the dark immediately assume a dangerous aspect. It
was unfortunate that the Prince's inability to see his cousin,

except in secret, invested their clandestine meetings, whether he liked it or not, with the character of a conspiracy. One does not go out at night by a back way wrapped up to the ears, or jump into a *fiacre* to throw a spy off the scent, or steal into a house by the servant's entrance, for the purpose of discussing the weather with a friend. The discussions between the Prince and the Archduke touched upon the gravest affairs of the State.

So far as the Prince was concerned, the primary object of the conversations was a thorough investigation of their problems. He desired to examine the theories of the Liberals with a man he could trust, with one of his own family. It was his idea to prepare the ground for the future. The Archduke, who was inclined to take risks and also enjoyed intrigue, had a more immediate aim. He was whole-heartedly for action, and was always straining at the leash. Still, he instinctively felt the Prince's passive opposition and realized that he was very far from considering direct action.

He therefore proposed to implicate him by gradually involving him in a network of intrigue, without letting him be aware of his ultimate purpose. The Crown Prince would thus be compromised, and, at the appointed moment, would be compelled to play the principal part.

The Archduke knew his cousin. He must not counter him, but play upon the fits of anger which would inevitably follow the check of his attempts to effect military reforms. The General Staff would consider the Prince's plans with deference, but would not deviate an inch from their course. That would provide John Salvator with an opportunity for a bolder thrust and enable him to carry his plan a stage further.

If the Prince did not see right through his cousin's game, he was shrewd enough to guess that John Salvator was working behind his back. How far would he venture? At the bottom of his heart Rudolph was not anxious to know, in case he might have to break with him. That he would have regretted.

Before the Prince's departure for Galicia, a slip of the
Archduke's tongue aroused his suspicions and put him on
his guard. While discussing the Prince's stay at Lemberg,
in alluding to the Chief Staff Officer of the Eleventh Army
Corps, he dropped the following remark:

'He is one of us. Perhaps you could say a word to him.'

'A word about what?' the Prince asked curtly.

'Oh! just a word of encouragement,' replied the Archduke,
seeing that he had gone too far.

The Prince did not press the matter further, although it
left him with a disagreeable impression.

In the train, the expression: 'He is one of us,' came back
to his mind and made him feel very uneasy. To his feverish brain, it had an extremely sinister meaning. 'One of us,'
that was exactly the expression that would be used in alluding to a conspirator. A conspirator! So there was a conspiracy, a secret understanding between the Archduke and
higher officers of the Army on the active list?

Suddenly he had a glimpse of what was going on behind
his back. He saw that his cousin's ostensible interest in
theories cloaked a practical mind, and he guessed it was his
purpose to have an armed force ready to use when circumstances were propitious. Nothing could be more odious to the
Prince than a mutiny or a military *coup d'état*, for he was a
soldier and loyal to the core.

Hitherto, he had imagined rather naïvely that one could
talk of anything with impunity. Now he saw that, sooner or
later, words will inevitably be translated into deeds. The idea
that he, the heir to the throne, and a field-marshal, might be
the ringleader of a mutiny, maddened him. Military insur-
rections might suit the Russians, who were semi-Asiatic, and
shifty and cruel. The history of their dynasty was full of
such revolts. But he, a Hapsburg, never! He became more
and more incensed with his cousin for attempting to
manoeuvre him into a position which could only lead to dis-
honour. He decided to have the matter out directly he returned to Vienna, and, if necessary, to break with him.

During his short stay in Galicia the matter galled him more and more. He could not help scanning the face of the Chief-of-Staff of the Army Corps, and wondering whether he looked like a traitor. Yet, by a curious inconsistency, his manner toward him was most genial.

He arrived back in Vienna in the morning, tired out. In the heavy correspondence awaiting him he found several irritating letters. There seemed always to be obstacles in his path. He had an exceedingly unpleasant meeting with his wife. For the time being the Princess had adopted the role of victim. She spoke little, and sighed a great deal. 'There's nothing natural about the woman,' he thought. 'I almost think I prefer her in one of her tempers.' All of this was not calculated to reduce the pressure on his nervous system.

There was, however, a pleasant moment, when Count Hoyos came to see him. He was a simple soul, without much imagination, and absolutely incapable of disloyalty. The Prince often invited him to hunt with him. The Count came to ask him to a supper party that evening at the Café Sacher.

'We shall be quite by ourselves,' he said, 'all men. You, Philip and myself. I have discovered a Tzigan girl such as you have never heard. Her name is Marinka; she has only just come to Vienna and is a little untamed, but she sings divinely.'

'My dear boy, I'm afraid I can't come,' replied the Prince. 'I'm tired out. I had to drink more than was good for me in Galicia. That seems to be part of my trade. And their Tokay was not too good. My whole day is taken up with business, I shall go to bed early.'

Count Hoyos replied with a laugh.

'That's a very noble resolution. But after a day of red tape, after your back has been put up a dozen times by those old fossils in the *Stuben Ring*, and after a ceremonial dinner at the Palace, you will be ready enough for a little relaxation in a quiet room at Sacher's. There will be nothing to worry you there, no ceremony, the best of wine, two or three nice creatures to look at, and then Marinka! I should be very surprised if she didn't please you.'

The Prince, however, was obdurate.

'She will have to sing to you tonight. I mean to try to get some sleep,' he said.

'Very well,' replied the Count, 'but if you find you can't sleep, you will know where to find us.'

The Prince had a most tedious day. At the dinner in the Palace in the evening, the Archduke Albrecht, the victor of Custozza, whose influence was still all-powerful at the War Office, was present. The old man was very loquacious, and irritated the Prince beyond measure. He remembered a saying of John Salvator: 'There is always some hope of coming to an understanding with your father; with Uncle Albrecht, never! And he holds the Army in the hollow of his hand. We shall have to get rid of him!'

Directly after dinner the Prince managed to escape. He went to his apartments for a moment, then, after Loschek had seen the coast clear, he went out alone by the small iron gate leading into the Schweizerhof. A *fiacre* was waiting for him at the corner of the Josephs-platz. He gave the driver an address, telling him to drive there as fast as possible.

A few minutes later the Prince got out in one of the busiest streets of Vienna, and turned off immediately into a side street. He entered by a back staircase a quiet looking house, pushed open a door on the ground floor, went up two flights, knocked at a dingy door, and was shown by an old man into a spacious flat, of which several rooms were lighted. It seemed to the Prince that, as he was passing, the door of one of the rooms was hastily closed, to enable two or three people to keep out of sight. This annoyed him, and he arrived in a state of irritation at a room temporarily arranged as an office, where he found his cousin John Salvator.

Since the Archduke's slip about the Chief Staff Officer of the Eleventh Corps, the Prince had decided to be careful and to endeavour to find out exactly how far John Salvator had committed himself. So he made an effort to control his temper, and the cousins began their conversation in an atmosphere of calm.

Milli Stubel was not there that evening. The Prince regarded this as a bad sign. John Salvator evidently intended to talk politics.

At that moment the Archduke found himself in a sufficiently delicate position. He had worked behind the scenes far more than his cousin was aware. The time had now arrived when it was necessary to prove to the hotheads of the party that the Crown Prince was on their side. He had, therefore, resolved to force his cousin's hand; but he knew he must proceed with the utmost wariness.

The Prince, for the moment, led the conversation. He spoke sympathetically of the officers of junior rank, who were mainly drawn from the middle classes. Well informed and acquainted with the burning political questions of the day, they were on the whole favourably inclined towards the Liberals.

'They are our most reliable support, Gianni,' he said, using his own special name for his cousin.

The Archduke replied, shrugging his shoulders:

'They will be on our side when the battle has been won, but we can't count on them to do the fighting. We must have storm troops for that.'

The Prince interrupted with a rather forced laugh.

'You don't seem to have forgotten the vocabulary of your old trade, Gianni. All your terms are drawn from soldiering. It sounds as if we were preparing a revolution.'

The last word produced an uncomfortable silence. The Prince gave a rapid glance at his cousin, who was not inclined to continue excepting on his own ground. He had his plan and led the conversation into another channel.

The Prince was getting impatient. He had the impression of being a plaything in his cousin's skilful hands. Meanwhile the latter, who had just sent for wine, was speaking of the difficulties inseparable from initiating a new movement on so wide a scale.

'One fancies one can control the pace. In practice, that's very far from the case. One is not dealing with a homogeneous mass, but with a mixture of heterogeneous elements. Some are too apathetic; they have to be stirred up. Others are too much excited. Let us call them the extremists. They have to be held back. It's no easy matter. There is another point. We have made promises to these people. A time comes when it's necessary to do something for them, or at least to let them have a glimpse of the goal. Otherwise, they drop out of the ranks.'

He continued for some time in this strain, getting a little closer to his objective. The Prince saw the line he was taking. He emptied his glass and listened, smouldering with anger, and becoming more and more incensed as his cousin's purpose became more clearly defined. Then a totally unexpected incident upset the Archduke's subtle plan.

A confused murmuring sound was heard coming from one of the other rooms in the flat. The Prince leaped to his feet; instinctively he felt in his hip pocket for his revolver.

'What is that?' he asked irritably.

The Archduke, signing to him not to move, was already disappearing through the door.

The Prince kept his revolver in his hand. The noise continued fitfully for a time, then there was silence. A few minutes passed.

The Archduke returned. There was a slight flush on his usually pale face, and a gleam of excitement in his eyes. He was smiling.

This time the Prince made no attempt to control his feelings. While waiting, he had grown more angry, and there was no note of friendliness in his voice.

'What is going on?' he demanded. 'There are men in the flat, and they are here on your invitation!'

He spoke as a man who means to be obeyed. John Salvator was under no misapprehension. He decided to face the matter squarely, but, with the elasticity of his race, replied in a voice which was almost comical:

'These damned extremists! I told you it was difficult to keep them quiet.'

'What are you driving at?' almost shouted the Prince. 'What have you promised those men in there?'

The Archduke, seeing an opening, interrupted him, and with the same tone of irony said:

'Nothing but a sight of you. Nothing more. You will not have to say a single word that might compromise your reputation. Just a few platitudes: "Gentlemen, I am delighted to see you. We are all working for the same ideal" – and so on. "Ideal" pleases you, I am sure. It's one of the favourite words of your vocabulary. No one can be hanged for using the word "ideal". It's only the people at the Hofburg who might find something suspicious about it. On the whole, I think you might risk it. That's all I ask you. And if that is too much, to show yourself would be sufficient.'

Instead of calming the Prince, this explanation irritated him the more.

'I can see through your double dealings,' he said. 'God only knows what you have schemed behind my back, and promised in my name. You are preparing a revolution. You have given your accomplices an undertaking that, when the day comes, I shall be at their head, and that they will march under my banner. How far have you gone? I have been left entirely in the dark. But now you find you have to let me into the secret, for your extremists are clamouring for proof that you have not been talking hot air, and that I am ready to back you. You think you can bring me on to the stage, just as a showman pulls the strings of a marionette, without even asking my permission. Very well, you have made a very great mistake. I am not with you.'

He strode up and down the room, looking wild and haggard. For a moment he was silent. The Archduke made no reply. He was determined to keep his temper and thought it wiser to let the Prince work off his fury.

'What have you been plotting?' continued the Prince. 'To stir up the Hungarians, the Czechs, or the Croatians to rebellion, to incite mutinies in the Army, to throw the whole Empire into confusion and bring it to the verge of ruin? You counted on me for that? This time I expect an answer, and a plain one.' He banged his fist on the table so violently that the wine was upset.

The Archduke replied with the utmost calm:

'By God, to throw the Empire into confusion would not be very difficult. You know, as well as I do, what the internal peace of the country is worth. As for bringing it to the verge of ruin, it is there already. When you are in a reasonable frame of mind, you think exactly as I do. So what is your rage about? I too love my country, but I am thoroughly alarmed at the state to which this imbecile Government has reduced it, and I am convinced we are heading for disaster. You agree with me about all these things. Then what is it that divides us? It is this. I say: "To save the Empire and the Throne, we must act, and without delay. Tomorrow will be too late. Otherwise there will come a cyclone that will destroy us all." And you, who are as convinced as I am that the present situation is fraught with deadly peril, you say: "Let us speak of the future, of the future, of the future." That and nothing more. But, Rudolph, don't you understand that the time for words is past? A solution that way is a little too simple, a little too easy. What are we to wait for? The death of your father? With his constitution he may easily live twenty years. Do you mean to wait twenty years, while all the people of the Dual Monarchy are watching, with their eyes fixed on you? Do you wish to be, in your turn, an old man with blunted feelings in whom every ideal is dead? So far as I am concerned, that is a form of suicide I do not intend to contemplate.'

The Prince did not stir. Everything the Archduke had just said he had said to himself a hundred times. Only with him it had been entirely a case of words. Now the words were becoming reality. In one of the adjoining rooms there were men, unknown to him, whom his cousin had brought there. That thought obsessed him. He was still shaking with rage. 'They can't play that game with me,' he kept repeating to himself.

'Whom have you there?' he almost shouted. 'For the moment I am not interested in your ideas. Tell me who is there.'

With a shrug the Archduke asked:

'Are you really anxious to know? There are officers there. I have no doubt that you know some of them. If you like, I will bring them into this room one at a time, and you can talk to them.'

'I have no intention of seeing them,' shouted the Prince, beside himself. 'Tell me their names.'

This time the attitude of the Archduke changed. He replied with marked coldness.

'That is precisely what I shall not tell you.'

The Prince guessed his cousin's thought. He moved threateningly towards him.

'What?'

John Salvator did not flinch.

'I think you are losing your head,' he said. 'You had better go home. The air of the Hofburg suits you. You have nothing in common with us.'

The Prince turned deadly pale. He raised his arm, as if to strike his cousin. He curbed himself, took several steps across the room and flung himself into an armchair.

There was a long and heavy silence. The Prince's eyes were closed. He saw in a kind of nightmare a deep hole before him; he felt himself sinking into it, until the slime choked him. The scene changed. He saw an officer, revolver in hand, who resembled himself as a brother, in a room yonder at the Burg. He seemed to hear the broken sounds of a struggle coming from adjoining rooms and corridors, and, from time to time, there arose cries of 'Long live Rudolph! Long live the Emperor Rudolph.' And he saw the officer holding out a paper to an old man, who was ghastly pale, and heard him say, 'Sign'. So clear was the vision that he shuddered.

'Impossible,' he cried.

The sound of his own voice startled him. Opening his eyes, he recovered. There, with his elbows on the desk and his head buried in his arms, was John Salvator. The Prince rose, went over to him, hesitated a moment, then gently placed his hand on his shoulder. John Salvator looked at him, and the Prince saw that there were tears in his eyes. The Prince could hardly speak for emotion, and in a hoarse voice said to his cousin: 'You are right, Gianni, I am a broken reed.' He added, almost inaudibly, 'I beg you to forgive me.'

'If it must be thus,' murmured the Archduke, 'I shall leave the country.'

'It will be best so,' said the Prince. 'My God! how I envy you!'

A moment later, at the corner of a neighbouring street, he got into the *fiacre* which had brought him there.

'The Café Sacher,' he said, 'as fast as you can drive.'

CHAPTER IV

NOTES FROM AN OCTOBER DIARY

At the Café Sacher.

HE PASSED WITH long rapid strides along the corridor leading to the private rooms at Sacher's. A *maître d'hôtel* hardly had time to get out of his way. He went into one of the rooms. The atmosphere was heavy with the perfume of flowers, of women, and of wine. Count Hoyos and his guests rose to their feet as he entered.

'We were hoping Your Imperial Highness would come, and have waited supper,' said the Count in his deep cheery voice. 'I think you know these lovely ladies,' he added, presenting two chorus girls who had already made a name for themselves. 'And this is Marinka.'

The woman to whom he referred looked unusually fragile. She had an amber skin, almond eyes, and raven black, glossy hair tightly braided round her small head. She kept a little in the background.

'She comes from the South of Russia,' he continued, 'but she lived in Bukovina for a time and speaks a decent German.'

The Tzigan girl gave the Prince the impression of being insignificant. He nodded to her pleasantly and held out his hand to a middle-aged man with a weather-beaten face and hair turning grey over the temples. This was his cousin, Prince Philip of Coburg, who usually accompanied him on shooting expeditions.

'Now let us have supper,' said the Prince. 'It is at last the hour for serious matters. Let us first drink to drive away dull care. Hoyos, give me a glass of vodka in honour of Marinka.'

He drained his glass eagerly and asked for another.

*   *   *

Late in the night the Tzigan girl sang to them. At her request half the candles had been blown out. A man had just entered the dim room. He was pale and sickly, and in a close-fitting jacket such as the Tzigans wore. Leaning against the wall, her head thrown back, a faraway look in her unfathomable eyes, Marinka sang. Her voice was of marvellous volume. Her sense of rhythm seemed to pour through the fibre of her body from her very soul. Whether she gave utterance to folk songs of her native land, in which rapture mingles with despair, or to popular melodies of the day, she stirred her listeners to the utmost depths of their being.

Nothing could have been more in keeping with the Prince's mood. A deep unquenchable pain gnawed at his heart. How could life ever be the same again, after that scene with Gianni? Happiness, for him, was glimpsed only to be dashed from before his eyes. Yet Marinka's voice brought oblivion, the supreme relief. '*Un narcotique venu du fond de l'Inde,*' he thought. He could not bear her to stop. When at last she was silent, he drew her toward him and took her hand. They remained thus some time without speaking. Suddenly she kissed him lightly on the forehead, saying only one word:

'*Biedni!*' [1]

'What does that mean?' asked the Prince.

She made no answer. Nobody knew its meaning.

'It's Russian,' said Hoyos, 'but the only word of Russian I know is *nitchevo*, and I'm not quite sure what that means.'

*   *   *

A strange visit.

The following morning, about nine o'clock, while Loschek was busy tidying the Prince's salon, he had a great surprise.

The door of the room was gently opened. It was the Empress. She was quite alone. She was dressed in black and carrying a small fan. It was the first time she had ever come

---

[1] Poor fellow.

to her son's apartments. That she was unaccompanied was even more unusual. The old servant, who had known the ways of the Hofburg for thirty years or more, could hardly believe his eyes. It was wellnigh incredible that the Empress, without either a lady-in-waiting or a companion, should have crossed the long range of corridors and salons between the Prince's private suite of rooms and her own.

With quick light steps, in spite of her fifty years, she moved towards Loschek, who bowed to the ground.

'His Imperial Highness is not here?' she asked.

'His Imperial Highness is giving an audience,' replied Loschek. 'If Your Majesty so desires, I will inform His Highness of Your Majesty's presence.'

'No,' said the Empress, 'I do not wish to disturb him. It is you I have come to see, Loschek.'

The old man looked at her in amazement. This was beyond his comprehension.

The Empress continued:

'How is my son, Loschek? You have always looked after him, you know him as well as I do myself. For some time he has looked unwell. What is the matter? Is it influenza? Or, perhaps, overwork?'

'It's overwork, Your Majesty,' said Loschek, 'it's that and nothing else. His Highness is over-tired; that is all. There is nothing more – but he sleeps badly. He is very restless at night. I can see it plainly, when I go into his room in the morning. Sometimes he moans in his sleep. It wrings my heart to hear him. And it wrings my heart to wake him in the morning. But I have my orders. He wouldn't forgive me if I let him be late. He goes to bed too late, that's true, but his life drives him to it.'

He stopped talking. The Empress had listened, without moving, to the old retainer's long speech, with her face partly hidden by her fan. But when he added: 'His Highness will be very touched to hear of Your Majesty's visit,' she stopped him, saying: 'I do not wish you to mention my visit,

Loschek. I forbid it. Perhaps I shall come again one of these days.'

She took several steps, and looked round the room. Her eyes rested on the desk. In the centre, behind the inkstand, was the skull. She shrugged her shoulders. She went nearer and looked at the grinning skull carefully; then slowly, as if regretfully, she turned away. On the side of the writing table lay a revolver. Pointing to it, she said:

'You leave that lying there! I don't like that! I don't like that!'

With these words she vanished so rapidly that Loschek had not time to open the door. Behind her there lingered a faint scent of heliotrope. When the old man was alone, his legs gave way, and he fell rather than sat on a chair. He needed time and quiet to fathom the scene that had just taken place.

*   *   *

In the Prater.

The weather that year in the latter part of October was magnificent. In the Prater the leaves of the trees had hardly begun to turn, and it was thronged with gay carriages and people on horseback, anxious to make the most of the weather before winter set in in earnest. Society and business people, highborn ladies and fashionable actresses were there.

A smart victoria was seen to pass. Its sole occupant, a Tzigan woman, seemed out of keeping with the scene. She sat looking straight in front of her. Very few knew who she was. It was whispered that she came from Russia, that her name was Marinka, and that the Crown Prince admired her.

Almost every afternoon Baroness Vetsera drove slowly up and down the main avenue. Judging by the number of people with whom she exchanged greetings, she was one of the most popular women in Vienna. Marie was always with her, sometimes her eldest daughter, too.

But he, whom Marie hoped to see, was never there. He might be shooting, or else at Prague, or Budapest or Gratz;

he might be in Vienna; he was anywhere but in the Prater. For over a fortnight he had not been at the Imperial Theatre, which Marie attended regularly when the Prince was in residence at the Hofburg. She had seen him once, only once, since her eventful conversation with Countess Larisch. At that moment she was indescribably happy.

Alas! A week had passed without her setting eyes on him, and she was back in the depths of despair. She, who lived in the gayest and most cheerful house in Vienna, felt herself lonely and a burden to herself and those around her. She took no part in the conversation, unless the Prince's name was mentioned, but she noticed that people, when speaking of him, often lowered their voices. At first this worried her. Surely, somebody must suspect her feelings for him. No, that was not possible. Countess Larisch was so true a friend that her loyalty could not be doubted. An explanation must be sought elsewhere. What was there in the Prince's life that had to be so carefully concealed? Unfortunately Countess Larisch had just left for her country estate, and Marie dared not put a question in writing about the matter. If Madame Vetsera had noticed a letter in her friend's handwriting, she would very likely have opened it.

So poor Marie's life was full of worry and misgivings. She was in love, and without hope. Yet, even had she wished it, she could not have freed herself from her infatuation.

One day, she went to the Prater a little more hopefully. The Crown Prince had been two days in Vienna, and had not been out riding. It was now nearly three weeks since they had met. Had he no wish to see her? Marie smiled sadly at her thought. How could she suppose that a Prince, who was so handsome and in such request, still remembered her?

The sun was getting low. Madame Vetsera's landau had driven twice down the main avenue. Evidently the Prince was not coming. Marie felt chilled all over. Her mother, noticing how pale she looked, asked whether she was cold. Marie, seeing an opportunity for prolonging the drive, said that she was so, and asked permission to take a short walk with her sister. The Baroness readily acquiesced, but herself remained in the landau. She thoroughly disliked walking.

Marie and Hanna took the path through the wood skirting the main avenue, while the landau went on slowly. Just as they reached a spot where the path deviated a little from the edge of the wood, they suddenly came upon an officer on horseback. He was leaning forward to speak to a lady whom the girls could not see clearly. He had his back turned to them, yet, as she drew closer, Marie's heart beat faster. When the girls came up with them, they were obliged to make a slight detour to avoid the horse.

Just at that moment the officer sat up in his saddle and Marie recognized the Prince. Her confusion may be imagined. She lowered her eyes, and raised them immediately. The Prince was looking at her; he was only a few paces away; she had never been so near him before. She noticed at the same time, that the woman to whom he was speaking was the strange looking person she had noticed in the victoria. Consumed by feelings she could not define, fearing above all to appear indiscreet, she turned away.

She hardly had sufficient strength to go on, or to answer the questions of her sister, whose curiosity was greatly piqued by this surprising encounter. They had not gone more than fifty yards, when they heard the sharp trot of a horse in the avenue. It was the Crown Prince passing them, and he was looking in their direction. Marie thought he made an almost imperceptible bow.

CHAPTER V

A LETTER

A FEW DAYS later, the Prince returned late at night to the Hofburg. Instead of going to rest, he lighted a cigarette and stretched himself in an armchair, a prey to deep depression. The narcotic from the mysterious East had lost its power. He must look elsewhere for relief. But where? Was there no longer balm in Gilead? The grinning skull, with the lamp-light shining on its polished surface, caught his attention. He wondered what life was like beyond the grave. His mind played round the idea of death. For long it had had no terrors for him. 'Peace, perfect peace—' but it was the last solution of all. Before adopting it, he must attempt all the others.

Then John Salvator and charming Milli Stubel came into his mind. They had found happiness! This started a new train of thought. Suddenly he went to his desk and wrote a short note. He then called Loschek and instructed him to have the letter delivered before nine in the morning, by special messenger.

On retiring to rest, the Prince wondered whether the letter would reach its destination; perhaps he had done a stupid thing in acting on the spur of the moment. But he felt vaguely that he could not wait, and that the sudden inspiration that had prompted the letter was one of those that cannot be resisted.

Marie Vetsera had spent a miserable time since her last drive in the Prater. She had certainly seen the Prince there, but under what peculiar circumstances! In conversation with a woman for whom he apparently was not afraid to compromise himself. Once more pretty Marie, whom all

Vienna admired, felt herself utterly insignificant. With the modesty that was natural to her and was part of her charm, she had too low an opinion of herself and exaggerated the attractions of her rival. The latter's beauty seemed to her flawless. Had not the Prince specially noticed her?

Naturally the Prince's meeting with Marinka had not remained a secret. Marie had begged her sister not to talk about it, but in vain. Hanna was quite unable to resist telling her friends such a piquant tale. Of course the story became the subject of countless comments. Marie learned that the Prince was madly in love with the beautiful Tzigan girl, and that he was with her constantly, even in the Prater! What little piece of embroidery was not added? It was whispered that matters had become so strained between the Prince and the Princess that she had threatened to leave him and return to Belgium. This piece of news contained nothing in itself disagreeable to Marie. It was the circumstances connected with it that were so painful. It was even stated, of course without the slightest justification, that the Emperor had intervened.

Such was the atmosphere of gossip that Marie breathed. It was poison to her. Countess Larisch was still at her country house, a long way from Vienna. In whom could she confide? Where could she find consolation? She could do nothing but weep in the arms of her old nurse, who was powerless to help her and terrified.

One morning, it was Monday the twenty-first of October, the old woman brought in her breakfast. For the last few days, being tired, Marie had breakfasted in bed. Her nurse pointed to a letter on the tray and said:

'There is a registered letter for you. I was alone downstairs when a special messenger brought it, so I took it in and signed for it.'

Marie looked at the letter in amazement. Her letters, as those of everyone in the house, were usually taken up to her mother's room. The envelope was addressed to 'Baronesse

Marie Vetsera.'[1] It had the Vienna postmark. Who ever had sent her a registered letter? It was the first she had received in her life. She tore open the envelope and read the contents eagerly. It was headed *The Hofburg*, with the Imperial arms below the address. She could not believe her eyes. The letter was as follows:

DEAR MADEMOISELLE VETSERA,

Will you do me the honour of meeting me in the Prater tomorrow, Tuesday? We could meet at about 4 o'clock at the quiet spot where I had the pleasure of seeing you the other day. My request may appear a little strange, but, having admired you for so long from a distance, I should like to have the privilege of making your acquaintance.

RUDOLPH, P.I.

Marie read the letter twice, so as to be quite sure of its meaning. Then she hurriedly hid it under her pillow. Her mother or sister might come in. What would they say? With her head on the pillow, almost against the letter, and her eyes wide open, she tried to think. But she was so excited that she could not collect her thoughts. Her brain kept repeating: 'He has written to me, he has written to me. The Crown Prince has written to Baronesse Marie Vetsera. Rudolph has written to Marie. He hasn't forgotten me after all. He wants to see me. He is making an appointment with me; that shows he loves me. Oh, I shall die of joy! In the Prater; we two alone in the Prater. Does he really love me? I expect I am only a distraction for him. That's only natural. Little matters. I love him; I am going to see him; I shall speak to him; I shall be alone with him.'

Then she grew a little calmer.

'The letter reached me only by a miracle,' she thought.

[1] In Austria the daughters as well as their mothers take the title. The mother's title was Baronin Vetsera, and Marie's Baronesse Marie Vetsera.

'Mamma looks at all my correspondence, and this letter slipped through. It seems like Providence.'

While she was in the middle of these thoughts, her old nurse came in for the breakfast tray.

'What's the matter with you, my child?' she asked.

Marie looked at her and said:

'I'm much too excited to eat. Please take away the tray. I am going to get up. I'm tired of my bed.'

The old nurse was very glad; she had not seen her so happy for fully six months.

'You've had a very nice letter, I see,' she said, taking away the tray.

As she was stooping for it, Marie whispered in her ear:

'He has written to me.'

The old woman nearly dropped the tray. Holding it in front of her, she said, shaking her head:

'So now you have begun to write to each other.'

Marie was already flitting about the room.

Only a little later, she found she had omitted to take into consideration a very simple little fact.

'But I can't go to the Prater,' she suddenly remembered. 'I am not allowed to go out by myself.'

Her expression suddenly changed. There was no hope in the matter. There was no way of her leaving the house alone, even for an hour. That meant that she would not see him or speak to him, that she would not walk at his side with his arm in hers! There was only one person in the world to whom she could apply in the circumstances, her dear Countess Larisch. If she had been there, the matter would have been easy. Madame Vetsera would readily have allowed Marie to go out with her. They would have started alone, just they two, and then, and then — But this was idle dreaming. The Countess was in the country. Such was Marie's life. She was always passing from the height of bliss to the depth of despair.

Practical ideas, to meet the situation, gradually took shape. First of all she must write to the Prince to explain that she was unable to meet him. And she must write without delay to Countess Larisch, imploring her to return to Vienna immediately. When she returned, what joys there were in store! The certainty of seeing the Prince so soon helped her to bear the terrible disappointment of not meeting him the next day. She took pen and paper. Without further hesitation, she wrote him the following letter:

YOUR IMPERIAL HIGHNESS,

I should have been only too happy to meet you in the Prater tomorrow. But I am very sorry that I shall be unable to come, as I am not allowed to go out without a chaperon.

If only Countess Larisch had been here, I am sure she would have brought me. I am writing to her by this post asking her to return to Vienna.

I am deeply distressed at not being able to come.

She did not know how to end the letter, so simply signed herself 'Marie'. When she re-read it, she thought it stiff and clumsy. But the more she thought about it, the more difficult it seemed to write one which satisfied her. Finally, she slipped it into an envelope and addressed it to the Crown Prince at the Hofburg, with indescribable pleasure, carefully following the instructions given by him in a postscript to insure its safe delivery.

Her letter to the Countess was less brief. It was nothing but a paean of joy, four pages long, with variations, and mingled with entreaties to return to Vienna at once. After she had written it, she thought the letter would not reach the Countess in her estate at Pardubitz until the following day, and decided to send a telegram. Her old nurse was sent with it to the telegraph office without delay.

CHAPTER VI

3RD NOVEMBER, 1888

COUNTESS LARISCH arrived in Vienna two days after she had received Marie's letter. She had had a letter from the Prince, too, begging her to return as soon as possible. Being exceedingly anxious to oblige him, she decided to start at once. She reached the capital on All Saints Day, and stayed at the Grand Hotel as usual. There she found a note from the Prince, who was away for the day shooting, asking her to call and see him the following morning about mid-day. She was amused to find a second letter from Marie, who was eagerly expecting her at the Salezianer Strasse, and said that she would probably be alone after the morning Mass. The Countess accordingly walked over to see her about eleven.

Marie could no longer contain her excitement. The prospect of seeing the man who had filled her thoughts for every minute of the last six months was at last to be realized. She did not wonder what their meeting would be like; it was enough that she was to see him, to hear his voice, to feel the touch of his hand. What more could her heart desire? She flung her arms round the Countess's neck, and chattered incessantly without letting her say a word. She was in ecstasy when she heard that the Prince had written and asked the Countess to call.

'May I come with you?' she ventured.

The Countess smiled.

'You're not thinking of going to the Hofburg, surely!' she said. 'That would be a little too risky. One of the side avenues of the Prater, perhaps. But what are you going to ask next?'

Before the Countess left, it was agreed that she would try

to arrange a meeting between eleven and twelve o'clock, as Madame Vetsera would be more likely to allow Marie to go out in the morning.

The next day the Prince was able to spare the Countess only a few minutes. He thanked her for having gone to so much trouble for him, but spoke in the ironical tone he often used to her.

'The country is not good for you, Marie,' he said, 'you are a woman with whom town life agrees. Confess that I have saved you from being bored. With me, the contrary is the case; towns do not suit me at all. But I am obliged to spend my life in them. There is nothing more fatiguing.'

He stretched himself, lighted a cigarette, and continued:

'I should love to see your little friend. I passed her the other day in the Prater. She's extremely pretty, and so young! Her beauty is the kind one doesn't see every day. I should like to see her closer. She's worth it. ... You must bring her here, Marie.'

The Countess laughed outright.

'What! Calmly bring her, a young girl, straight in here? Surely you are not thinking of that, my dear Rudolph! The risks are far too great.'

The Prince made a mental note that she spoke only of the risks of arranging the meeting. He saw that he had gained his point, and had only to reassure her.

'Would you prefer your own apartment at the Grand Hotel?' he asked. 'In my opinion one might as well choose a public place at midday! The Hofburg, if one sets to work the right way, is the safest place in Vienna. You will see no one but myself; so come, both of you, tomorrow morning. Nothing could be simpler. Bratfisch will be waiting for you a few minutes before twelve in the street behind the Grand Hotel, and will take you to the Josephs-platz. Then you pass under the archway. Only a few steps from there, on the right, you will see a small iron postern gate ajar. If you push the gate open you will find Loschek, who will bring you here by a private way, in perfect safety.'

On the Countess protesting further, he stopped her.

'Say yes, Marie. I know you are such a very charming person, I am sure you will oblige me.'

His tone was quizzical. She did not quite know what to make of it, but had to be satisfied. She saw Madame Vetsera later in the day, and asked her to let Marie go shopping with her in the morning. It so happened that Marie, not having a good photograph to give the Prince, had already made an appointment with the photographer. And Baroness Vetsera, who was very short and stout, was delighted at the idea of escaping a climb up the photographer's four flights of stairs.

'I am really very much obliged to you,' she said to the Countess, 'for saving me that terrible climb. Please see that he doesn't make Marie look too much of a ninny. And be sure you make her laugh. But whatever you do, don't let her out of your sight; she's the most precious thing I have.'

On Saturday morning the Countess was at the Salezianer Strasse before half-past ten. Marie was radiant and bursting with excitement. The Countess complimented her in the presence of the Baroness, who looked at her daughter with pride.

On the way, Marie was rather silent. The taking of the photograph proved to be rather a lengthy affair. She was taken in three positions; one with her green felt hat and fur coat, another in evening dress, and a third with her hair down.

'How tedious it is,' she kept saying to Madame Larisch, and, 'He is sure to think it hideous.'

At other moments she felt delighted at the thought of soon being able to give him a photograph.

'Make me look as beautiful as you can,' she said to the photographer. She added, laughing, 'Still, people must be able to recognize me.'

She kept looking at her watch. It would never do to keep the Crown Prince waiting. At last they were at the Hotel, a little before midday. They left it by the back way without raising suspicions. Bratfisch, installed on his box, was waiting for them as arranged. Although the chances of being seen in the dark landau were very slight, they took the precaution of hiding their faces in their boas.

In less than five minutes, Bratfisch brought them to the spot, near the Hofburg, mentioned by the Prince. Twenty yards farther, to the right they saw a postern gate ajar. They pushed it open and were received by Loschek. They followed him along narrow passages, climbed staircases, and crossed empty salons. 'It is a deserted palace,' thought Marie, 'Prince Charming's palace.' So great was her confidence in the Prince that she had no misgivings. He had arranged everything, so she would be quite safe.

Finally, they reached a door which Loschek opened. They were in a reception-room furnished in the chilly style of the Hofburg. From a neighbouring room they heard a voice, his voice, saying:

'Only a few more steps, ladies. I am in here.'

All at once Marie found herself face to face with the Prince, who held out his hand. She curtsyed almost to the ground.

The Countess laughed and said:

'You would not have made a deeper curtsy to the Empress, Marie.'

But the Prince, without taking further notice of his cousin, led Marie to a low armchair near a settee.

'Make yourself comfortable there, Mademoiselle,' he said. 'You are young enough to be able to bear the light. I have admired you from a distance for so long, you must let me look at you a little closer today.'

Each word came to Marie like a caress. She was not afraid to look into the Prince's eyes. They seemed to her gentle and mocking.

A triangular conversation began. Marie, to her great surprise, did not feel the least embarrassment. For six months she had communed in her mind with the Prince, had made him a thousand confidences, and had had no other intimacy than this. Now that she was in his presence their intercourse continued. Even the presence of the Countess was no hindrance. Had she not often spoken to her of the Prince?

Yet something she had not experienced in her dreams, she found disturbing. It was feeling the Prince's eyes upon her. His gaze scarcely left her. Now it was on her brow, now on her cheek, now on her lips; his eyes wandered over her whole figure. And always it seemed a real contact, giving a light, burning sensation, which lasted for an instant then disappeared. The kind of delicious discomfiture it brought was at times strong enough to prevent her from following the conversation. Whenever there was an opportunity, she looked at him. He was more handsome than she had thought and more attractive. She found his smile irresistible. But she was alarmed at his fatigued appearance, and, although he tried to conceal it, at his preoccupied air.

He thanked the Countess for having brought Marie to the Hofburg.

'It's the only safe place,' said Marie ingenuously.

'The lion's den,' said the Prince with irony.

The Countess interposed:

'Marie imagines herself a tamer of wild beasts.'

'Don't laugh at me,' replied Marie. 'I only meant to say that anywhere else we would risk meeting someone, while here I feel perfectly secure.'

The Countess commented:

'There you have the girls of today, my dear Rudolph.'

As she was saying this, the Prince rose. Marie followed his example.

'No, no,' he said, 'don't get up. Please let there be no formalities between you and me. But I beg you to excuse me for a moment, I have something to say to my cousin.'

'Will you come with me for a minute?' he said, turning to the Countess.

He took her out by a small door in the wall, which Marie had not noticed. Marie was left alone, and at last had an opportunity for examining the room. It was the small salon next to the sleeping-chamber which the Prince had used for some time. She got up and walked over to the window. She was surprised to find that it looked on to the Amalien Hof, and was just opposite the Empress's apartments. That moment, for the first time, she realized that she was in the Imperial palace, in the same building as the Emperor and Empress. Until then she had been visiting a man, whose name, for her, was Rudolph.

She came back to the table. The skull caught her attention. 'How can he live with that horrible thing in the room?' she thought. Suddenly the scene of Hamlet with Yorick's skull passed through her mind. The Prince had been there too; and, for a moment, his face had appeared under the features of the unhappy Prince of Denmark. She had felt sorry for him; she felt sorry for him now. Presently she noticed the revolver. She had a horror of firearms. She could not bear the noise they made. Why did he leave it on his desk? She shrank back instinctively. At that moment the Prince returned, alone.

'Where is the Countess?' Marie asked.

The Prince noticed that there was no trace of anxiety, but only surprise in her voice.

'I had a little trouble in persuading her to spare us her presence,' he said smiling. 'But I know how to take her. She always finishes by doing what I ask.'

He drew a little closer to Marie.

'Since you have had the courage to come here—'

Marie interrupted:

'There was no need of courage, I assure you.'

She spoke so naturally that for a moment the Prince hesitated.

'I was wrong,' he corrected himself. 'Since you have honoured me by coming here, I do not wish to share your company with anyone. You know the English proverb: *Two is company: three is none.*'

'Oh! yes,' said Marie vivaciously, 'it is much nicer to be only two, to be quite truthful – and, as I so want you to know me exactly as I am, I have made up my mind to speak nothing but the truth to you – I hoped very much to see you alone. Only I didn't think it would be possible. And then, in the twinkling of an eye, you arrange everything as in a fairy story.'

The Prince was struck just as much by the tone of her voice as by her actual words. Never had a girl a voice or a heart of such crystalline purity. He was delighted that he had followed his whim in writing to her. Before, in similar cases, the disillusion had proved almost immediate. As soon as he was face to face with women he had been anxious to meet, their insipidity became apparent at once, and he felt a desire to send them away without further ado. But the moment this young girl arrived, he felt that she was gaining a hold upon him. It was quite clear that she was neither acting a part nor playing for effect. She had nothing to hide; she was just naturally herself. Nothing could be more entirely satisfying. She created an atmosphere in which he breathed more freely. And how lovely she was!

It gave him such pleasure to look at her, and listen to her chatter, that, for the moment, he confined himself to an occasional repartee. She was speaking of 'their past'.

'The first time I saw you,' she said, 'was the twelfth of April. What a beautiful day it was! That brings good luck, you know.'

'Do you think so?' he asked, with a doubting smile.

'Are you not happy?' asked Marie quickly.

'Oh! Don't let's talk about me,' replied the Prince. 'You are much more interesting. Have you, at least, been happy?'

'I really do not know,' said Marie, 'so please don't ask me. Sometimes I was on the heights, and sometimes in the depths of misery. So how can one tell?'

She told him about the days passed in ups and downs, and the Prince was astonished to learn that, in the life of this girl, who was feted on all sides, there had been no one but himself for the last six months; that the only things she counted were seeing him at the theatre or in the Prater, and that the greatest despair she had known had been that unfortunate trip to England.

'Unfortunate?' he queried. 'Why unfortunate? The summer is extremely pleasant in England, especially for young ladies.'

Marie hesitated. At last, she said:

'I am sure you will laugh at me. I cannot help it if you do. But I didn't want to leave Vienna; I didn't want to be far away—'

She stopped, and for the first time since she had been talking to him, she blushed and looked away. There was a moment of silence almost as pleasant to the Prince as the conversation he had found so delightful. He was surprised. Was it solely to hear the chatter of a pretty girl that he had brought her – with a certain amount of risk, after all – to the Hofburg? They were alone together for the first time. She loved him. He found her infinitely desirable, and they remained there talking like old friends. He thought of Count Hoyos, who cynically expected from women the only thing that, according to him, they had to give. Opportunities for them to meet would be rare, and the time of her visit was slipping away fast.

He looked at Marie. Her confusion added yet another charm to her young face. He felt an almost irresistible longing to hold her in his arms, to kiss her fresh lips, and to feel the contact of her virgin body against his own. Consumed with desire he rose, and using the same words as on similar occasions, he said:

'What am I thinking of? I haven't even asked you to take off your fur. It's hot in here. And, won't you show me your hair? I have heard it is magnificent.'

'Yes, if you like,' said Marie, rising.

She looked round for a mirror.

'Is there no mirror here?' she asked, laughing. 'Are you as Spartan as that?'

'You will find one in the next room,' he replied, showing her the open door of his sleeping apartment.

Marie went into the room, which was quite small and simply furnished. In a corner was a narrow bed.

'Is this your sleeping apartment?' she said. 'You can see how imaginative girls are. I expected to see a large double bed, a prince's bed, and a state bed.'

The Prince began to laugh.

'You are perfectly right. Such a room exists, but I infinitely prefer this one.'

Marie went over to the mirror. The Prince followed, and stood near her.

'I am sure it will be all straggly,' she said, 'and you won't like it.'

She removed her hat, and revealed the dark mass of her hair, raven-black with bluish lights in it. It was coiled on the nape of her neck.

As she was taking off her cloak, he came nearer to help her. Now he was almost touching her. He leaned over toward her. They looked at themselves together in the mirror. The Prince's eyes were burning; Marie's clear eyes were smiling at him tenderly. This girl, hardly more than a child, almost in a man's arms, showed no sign of alarm. He read in her eyes absolute trust and innocent happiness. She had no fear of him; he could do her no harm. At that moment she leaned against him with a movement so chaste that he quivered. His face was drawn, as if he were struggling with himself. He moved away rather abruptly. Marie ran over to him anxiously and took his hand.

'What is it? What's the matter?' she asked.

'Oh, it's nothing,' he replied. 'It's stupid of me. I hardly know, myself. I'm all right again now – but it's all your fault.'

He was smiling again, and his light-hearted tone reassured her. He walked up and down the room for a minute, went back to her, took her hand in his, and, looking right in her eyes, asked:

'Do you often perform miracles?'

Marie was so astonished that she did not know what to

reply. But the Prince was now gay and in high spirits, and seemed a different man.

He led Marie into the other room, made her comfortable on a settee, gave her a glass of port and sat down on a footstool at her feet. Now it was he who talked of anything and everything, and in such a cheerful humour that Marie was both surprised and delighted. He looked younger and the furrow between his brows had disappeared. Suddenly, he said:

'Have you no request to make?'

Marie looked at him in bewilderment.

'Yes,' he continued, 'everyone who approaches me has some request to make; for an appointment, for promotion, for a decoration, or simply for money. The mere fact of coming to see me stamps a man as a petitioner. So, I would like to know what I can do for you, who are the prettiest petitioner I have ever had the pleasure of receiving.'

'But I want nothing,' said Marie; 'haven't I today all my heart's desire?'

'Well, I did think of you,' he continued.

He went to his desk, opened a drawer, and came back with a little case, which he offered her.

Mute with astonishment, she looked alternately from the Prince to the case.

'Why don't you open it?' he asked.

She opened it.

'Oh! what a lovely ring!' she exclaimed, 'sapphire and diamonds, but I cannot possibly accept it. Oh! I would love to have it,' she continued hastily, being afraid that the Prince might misinterpret her feelings, 'but you see, I couldn't wear it at home.'

'Before refusing it, will you look at the inscription inside?' said the Prince.

She looked at it and read: '12th April, 1888.'

'Can it be true?' she said eagerly, looking into his eyes. 'I can hardly believe it.'

'You are not the only person with a good memory for dates,' he replied.

'Oh! I am so happy!' continued Marie. 'I shall wear it in my room, every evening when I pray for you, and all night, and then I shall dream about you.'

He was at her knees and she gently stroked him, mingling her caresses and words of endearment: 'How good you are! How I love you!'

At that moment, there was a slight scratching noise at the door. The Prince started up.

'That's my watchdog,' he said. 'We must leave each other now! I have a State luncheon. All right, Loschek,' he called louder, 'I can hear you.'

He turned toward Marie.

'What can I say to you?' he said. 'You came here like a good fairy, the fairy I used to dream about when I was a little boy. She was beautiful like you. She used to touch unhappy people with her wand, and, instantaneously, they forgot their troubles.'

He helped her on with her fur, and continued:

'Since you arrived the atmosphere of this room has changed. Are we really still in the Hofburg? Since you came I have no cares, I am no longer unhappy.'

It was the second time he used this word, and involuntarily he emphasized it, which gave it a pathetic sound. Marie began to tremble. The Prince's face had changed. He looked pale and worn, and had a look of anguish in his eyes.

'Must you really go?' he stammered. 'Promise me to come back – out of pity.'

The word was as unexpected by him as by her. He was distressed. For a moment he was unable to control his emotion. To hide it, he took Marie in his arms and rested his head on her shoulder. She could feel his hot, quick breathing on her neck.

'Don't leave me alone,' he murmured. 'You do not know how much I need you.'

His voice was husky with emotion, and had a humble

pleading tone. Could this be the heir apparent to a mighty empire, speaking thus to a girl of seventeen? Marie's heart bled for him, and tears came into her eyes.

'I am yours, my darling, for always,' she said. 'Do what you like with me.'

The Prince had already recovered. In a lifeless voice, as if ashamed of his weakness, he said:

'I leave tomorrow for Buda; I shall be there five days. Then there is a big shoot in the Vienna forest, at Mayerling. But I shall be back here at the end of the week. Let us meet then. My cousin will arrange it – Loschek is going to take you back to her. Now, one must take up one's burden again.'

He said this in the tone of a man hard pressed, buffeted and tossed on the surface of life. He pushed open the door. Loschek was there.

PART III

CHAPTER I

THE DANGEROUS PATH

AMID THE CHAOS of impressions and feelings that Marie took away with her that morning, the memory of the last few minutes passed with the Prince predominated. That sad, strange scene depressed her for a long time. She could hear his pleading voice, and feel his hot, laboured breathing on her neck. So, he was unhappy! She had guessed rightly. How could he be otherwise with the life he led? But she had not imagined his distress to be so great. Today, the very first time they had met, it had become clear that he had need of her – of her, Marie Vetsera. It seemed incredible! Yet, how could she doubt it? She was far away from him, and he was suffering. Joy and despair! She was burning to see him again and hold him in her arms. She reproached herself for not having been tender enough, and for her inability to console him. The poor words she had used seemed to her hopelessly inadequate. 'What will he think of me?' she said to herself, and, 'will he think me hard and unsympathetic?'

But a great wave of joy swept away all these doubts. All her anxieties vanished before one tremendous fact. He loved her! To be loved by Rudolph! Had she ever in her wildest dreams hoped for such a miracle? A month ago, only a week ago, he seemed so far, so far away. And yesterday he was at her knees, and his head had rested on her shoulder. Could it be possible? He had asked nothing more of her. She felt that thus she was closer to his heart, that she had won a greater victory. He had had other women in his arms. Had he spoken to any of them as he had spoken to her as she was leaving? She knew he had not, and she was infinitely proud of it! She had taken possession of the part of him that was most precious to her, and there she would have no rival.

But love knows no peace. Everything separated her from the Prince. How was she to see him? Night and day she was obsessed by that thought. She was not allowed to go out alone. Her mother always accompanied her, and would not trust her with a maid. There was only Countess Larisch. She, of course, would be a great help. But she had many calls on her time, and she lived a good deal in the country. The Countess could not be continually at her beck and call. If she were to risk going out in the absence of her mother and sister, she would place herself in the power of servants. If they were to tell her mother, she knew only too well what her fate would be; either to be sent away from Vienna, or, worse still, to be sent back to the convent until a husband was found for her.

Her kind old nurse could be of no assistance. At the most she could help her in sending or receiving letters. For the time being, even that was impossible. In the fever of parting from the Prince, she had forgotten to arrange with him about corresponding. She must not forget next time. But when would that be? Never had a week seemed longer.

Countess Larisch had gone back to the country for a few days, though she had promised to return the same day as the Prince. So there was no one to whom Marie could open her heart. She had made up her mind not to mention her visit to her old nurse, to whom, hitherto, she had confided all her hopes and sorrows. This time the matter was too serious. Not a soul must know what she was doing.

But grief, no more than joy, accommodates itself to silence. In less than forty-eight hours she felt the need to unbosom herself. She could not resist showing her old nurse the ring. The old woman was thoroughly alarmed, and her fears supplied her with strength to speak to Marie and point out the abyss for which she was heading.

'Where are you drifting, my child?' she said. 'No good can come of this. Our Princes are spoiled, you know. They pluck the flower that pleases them. They fling it away – and then they take another. What better do you expect? He won't marry you. But you, my child, your heart is so tender; you will suffer.'

She took Marie's hand and kissed it. Marie saw how grieved she was. But she was not in a mood to let sadness get the upper hand. She laughed and whispered in the old woman's ear:

'You don't know him, Nanny. And if you were twenty you would do the same.'

At last, on the Friday, Countess Larisch called on Madame Vetsera. The Prince had returned to Vienna the preceding evening; Marie knew that. But would he, could he, see her on Saturday? The Countess soon put her out of her suspense. She asked the Baroness to allow Marie to go out with her on the following afternoon.

'She is such good company,' she urged, 'and I have no one to go out shopping with. Please let her come with me. I promise to bring her back in good time.'

This time, Madame Vetsera did not agree at once, not that she was in the least suspicious of her friend, but she had herself planned to go out with Marie. With her usual good nature, however, she agreed on a compromise. So it was arranged that the ladies should meet at five o'clock for tea at the Grand Hotel. . . .

*   *   *

Marie was again in the Hofburg, in the room which looks on to the Amalien Hof. The Countess, on leaving her at the little postern gate, had said, with a trace of irony:

'You are so grown up now, Marie, that I can let you go alone.'

The tone of the remark made Marie feel uncomfortable. What did her friend think? She blushed faintly at her thought, as she followed Loschek through the labyrinth of passages and staircases.

The room into which Loschek ushered her was empty. He

said that the Prince would come in a minute, and withdrew. It was beautifully decorated with azaleas and white chrysanthemums. This delicate attention was greatly appreciated by Marie. 'He has so much to do,' she said to herself, 'yet he found time to think of that!' The skull on the table stared out of its eyeless sockets. Marie approached it. She could not become reconciled to the idea of the Prince living in daily proximity with death. And that revolver always there! They were sinister companions! Still she plucked up courage and laid her hand on its shining surface. Its chilliness made her shudder.

'Are you not afraid of it?' asked a cheerful voice behind her.

She started. The Prince had come right up to her without her hearing. He was in mufti; she had never seen him in it before.

'Are you still the Crown Prince?' she asked, with her charming smile. 'I hardly recognized you.'

'Would you like me to go and change into uniform?' he asked. 'But I was so glad to get out of it for an hour,' he added.

She looked at him.

'Oh, no. Please don't go away. I like you just as well like that.'

He took her in his arms.

'You are like a ray of sunshine in this gloomy room,' he whispered.

'You keep bad company,' she said, looking at the skull, 'and there is that thing, too.'

She pointed at the revolver.

The Prince shrugged his shoulders.

'That is for the risks of the trade,' he said. 'Don't forget, my child, that first of all I am a soldier. I was dressed up in my first uniform at the age of four, when they turned me out all complete as a Uhlan! At twelve, I carried a revolver as part of my first subaltern's equipment. That's how I was brought up. You must make allowances for an unfortunate soldier.'

How Marie loved this bantering tone. Snuggling in his arms, she listened, in the seventh heaven of delight.

Now, he was talking about the skull.

'There's nothing terrifying in it,' he said. 'It was a poor devil's—'

'Did you know him?' she asked anxiously.

'Oh! no,' he replied. 'I simply mean he was a poor devil like the rest of us. No doubt he had a nagging wife, and aching teeth and his life was an intolerable burden. Then, one day, no more nagging wife, no more troubles, peace. Is there anything terrible in that? I can think of nothing more comforting.'

He leaned over her and looked into her blue eyes that were fastened on his own.

'We won't talk about it any more,' he said. 'It's all very well when I'm alone, and haven't your sweet face to look at.'

He took her over to the couch, and helped her to remove her cloak and hat.

'This is your kingdom,' he said, 'and I am your subject. You are just as safe here as in the Salezianer Strasse.'

An hour passed as in a dream. The Prince had never been gayer or in better spirits. He told her about his shooting expeditions; he had begun them when quite a small boy, and had always found them a delight.

'These expeditions,' he said, 'first made me love nature. One cannot learn the ways of nature when one has been brought up in a garden or a park. How I pity town children, both rich and poor. To know the lure of the forest, one must have roamed in it as a child, have seen dawn break, have dozed in a glade in the noonday heat, and have heard its mysterious voices at nightfall.'

Marie could have listened to him forever. 'Could anyone be more human or more natural?' she said to herself. 'I was not mistaken in him. I am the happiest woman in the world, when he is near me.'

When he stopped, she asked:

'Couldn't you take me just once into the forest? It's not far from Vienna. If you could spare two hours—. But I'm asking too much. Besides, in the winter it's not so beautiful.'

'The forest is always beautiful. In the different seasons it's a different beauty, that's all. Yes! We will go one day together into the *Wiener Wald*.'

'We should lose ourselves! I should be frightened, but you would protect me.'

'And we should never come back.'

They passed the afternoon in chatting like this. When it was time for Marie to go, she exclaimed:

'But I have only just come!'

The Prince looked at his watch, and could hardly believe his eyes.

'Can two hours have flown already?'

The tears were very near Marie's eyes.

'Must I go already? Keep me a little longer. But I expect you've had enough of me.'

Yet that afternoon, on which nothing particular occurred, was graven on their memories as the happiest either of them had ever spent.

Difficult days were in store for them. The following week the Prince had to go to Prague, and two days he was out shooting. But, inconceivable bad luck, during the four days he was in Vienna, the Countess was detained on her estate. The Prince was waiting for Marie in the little paradise at the Hofburg, while she fluttered in her mother's salon like a bird against the bars of a cage. Could any fate be more dreadful?

Still, she received two enchanting letters from him, that relieved her durance. They were addressed to the old nurse, who had never in her life had so much correspondence. The Prince wrote her a note from Prague. It was very short, but worth more than a whole ream: 'How can I live without you?'

The second was from Vienna, and its tone was rather depressed. He complained of worries, but without entering into details. His wife, perhaps! By this time Marie hated her. How could that Belgium woman be so stupid as to have failed to keep her husband's love, and wicked enough to ruin his life? She had been threatening to leave him for over a year. Why didn't she go back to her own country? The furrow on Rudolph's brow would soon disappear then.

Marie replied to both letters. She addressed hers to Loschek and sent them by special messenger.

'I love you,' she wrote, 'but I am so unhappy. I long to be everything to you, and I can be so little.' She deplored the absence of Countess Larisch. 'And when she is back, perhaps you will have gone! How I hate it when you are away from Vienna. If anything happened to you, what should I do?'

There were four pages in this strain.

She saw him one night at the opera, when *Tristan and Isolde* was being played. She had given the most anxious thought to her toilet, and had asked her mother to lend her some jewels. It was not usual in Vienna for girls to wear jewels. A simple enamel cross was all that was given them before their marriage. But Baroness Vetsera had lived in the East, and in the diplomatic world where there is more latitude in such matters. She was proud of Marie's beauty, and raised no objection to her request. Marie chose a diamond crescent for her hair. Oh! how she regretted not being able to wear Rudolph's ring. She kissed it before starting for the opera. She was dressed in white *crepe de Chine*, as she knew he liked her in white. The Crown Princess was to be present. Marie was determined to outshine the other women there that night.

The Countess had placed her box, which was near the Imperial box, at Madame Vetsera's disposal. Marie enjoyed a great success. The crescent created quite a sensation. She was delighted during the interval when her friends came and crowded round her, singing her praises. At that moment the Crown Prince and Princess and the Princess of Coburg arrived. Almost at once the Prince turned and looked in the direction of Madame Vetsera's party. Although he was not very far from them, he used his opera glasses. He made a slight sign of admiration which was not noticeable except by her. This time Marie did not blush. A moment later – they must have spoken of her in the Imperial box – she had the satisfaction of seeing the two Princesses look at her through their glasses. A little later, Marie looked at them. Neither of them was beautiful or elegant. The Prince, who was sitting behind them, seemed to belong to another race. 'What can they have in common?' thought Marie, and her heart was wrung at the thought that it was the fate of the man she loved to be bound for life to that woman.

She felt sad during the remainder of the evening. Her surroundings were painful, and seemed to bring out in strong relief the obstacles between her and the attainment of her desire. They were under the same roof, yet there was an infinite distance between them. He was not at liberty even to come over and chat to her, like the other men she knew. Their love was no ordinary one. They had that rare and indescribable spiritual affinity which unites men and women more closely than any legal bond, and there they found confronting them a mass of conventions, absurd, rigid, antiquated, unreal and inexplicable, which had assumed shape in the course of centuries, until they formed an impregnable barrier. They would never see each other except furtively, like thieves.

*   *   *

On the stage, Tristan was dying abandoned; Isolde arrived to join him in death. Is there no other refuge for unhappy lovers but death, the eternal refuge?

Marie wept bitter tears half through the night.

A line from the Prince next morning restored her to life: 'You were the most beautiful woman in the theatre last night ... R.' It was written on the note-paper of the Café Sacher.

CHAPTER II

STACCATO

A WEEK PASSED by. Countess Larisch had at last returned to Vienna and expected to remain there until New Year's Day. But the Prince had every day filled. Never had the drudgery of his rank seemed so irksome. He had now, in his life, an all-absorbing interest; but his time was not his own, and he rarely had a moment's freedom until the evening, too late to see Marie. One afternoon, however, he was able to arrange a meeting. The Countess escorted Marie to one of the side walks of the Prater and left them together.

It was already twilight. The Prince, wrapped up to the ears in an officer's cloak, put his arm in Marie's and led her at a brisk pace along one of the paths running into the wood. He walked so quickly that she was almost obliged to run to keep up with him. He did not slow down until they were in the middle of the thicket.

'If we have been seen,' he said, 'we shall have thrown the spies off the scent by this time. I am watched on every side. The superintendent of police, the Prime Minister and my wife, all have me followed. I am tracked like a wild animal. It's a hateful life, my little Marie! And you are not afraid of me! I wonder you don't avoid me.'

He spoke jerkily; his breath came in gasps. He said that his enemies would not rest until they had brought him down. And he complained of exhausting headaches. He became more and more agitated. In spite of the increasing darkness she could see his eyes burning in his deadly pale face.

She was seized with terror and pity alternately. What would be the end of it? Would his nerves give way under the strain? He seemed feverish; she was sure he would fall

ill. She dared not interrupt him, yet, she must try to calm
him.

Without saying a word, she quietly took his hand in hers.
The touch of her firm cool hand had its effect. Gradually
he grew calmer. At last he was quiet. The pressure of her
hand brought solace and gave him courage. It conveyed
still more; it told him that she would stand by him through
thick and thin, through life and in death.

Night was upon them. At times a branch whipped their
faces.

'We must leave each other soon, Marie,' he said tenderly.
'At night the Prater is more dangerous than the forest.'

He steered her through the darkness with unerring skill.
Soon they could see the outline of the trees. They were
nearing the edge of the wood.

'The Countess's brougham is over there,' he said, pointing
to some carriage lights not far away. 'Am I not a good
guide? Think of that, and forgive me for everything else.'
He was still trembling. Suddenly he took her in his arms and,
for the first time, kissed her lips passionately. He left her,
going off with long rapid strides in a direction away from
the waiting carriage. Marie slowly rejoined the Countess.
The Prince's kiss burned her. The flame it had kindled
would never die out.

*   *   *

Time was flying. Marie lived in a continual fever, a life of
waiting daily for an unexpected letter which arrived at last,
of arranging meetings in the face of countless difficulties, of
catching a passing glimpse of one another at the opera or in
the Prater, of making sure of the Countess's presence at the
necessary times, of scanning anxiously the headlines when
'he' was travelling to see that an attempt had not been made
on his precious life, of showing a smiling face, when her
heart was torn by anxiety. A daily life, moreover, of con-
cealing all signs of her passion, of appearing unconcerned,

of speaking or laughing with her people and friends about things in which she had lost all interest. And every day there was the drive, the going out into the world, the dances when she had to listen patiently to unwelcome attention; and all the while a persistent hammering in her brain: 'Where is he at this moment? Has he forgotten me? I love him!'

Whenever Marie had a spare moment and was alone with her thoughts she deliberately evaded every question of the future: 'Where is one drifting? Where will this end?' Ah, who listens to the whispers of prudence, when the present is upon one, hustling, overpowering, enchanting, like some strange tyrant, with a rose in one hand and in the other a lash?

Yet, even in her happiest moments, she was seized with fits of despondency. And often, after lying awake for hours, she fell asleep with tears in her eyes.

The Prince's health was beginning to fail seriously. The Empress's doctor came to see him – a few days before, the Empress had had a few minutes' secret conversation with Loschek. Doctor Wiederhofer had been present at his birth and, knowing the weaknesses and defects inherent in his constitution, fully recognized that in spite of his robust appearance, it was essential for the Prince to be very careful. The Doctor had gained his confidence, and that morning they were smoking a cigarette together with a bottle of port in front of them. He was developing one of his pet theories, that the great ones of the earth, on whose shoulders rest the heaviest responsibilities, are usually the least fitted to bear them. They had, as a rule, he maintained, weaker constitutions and greater calls upon them.

'I know,' he said, 'that I can speak freely to Your Highness. You are *au fait* with the latest theories of modern science, and I can say things to you which I should not venture to mention to other members of the Imperial family. Today the royal families of Europe are showing signs of strain. How could it be otherwise? Royalties lead far more strenuous lives than any private citizen. Their incessant and harassing duties allow them no relaxation. Moreover, this has been so for a dozen centuries or longer. Fatigue poisons are handed down from generation to generation and are cumulative. That in itself is a serious matter. And to complete my argument, there is the question of inter-marriage. For ten centuries no fresh blood has been introduced into the royal families. In Europe today you are all cousins. This is a highly dangerous state of affairs.'

'I have every reason to agree, Doctor,' said the Prince. 'I am often over-tired. And it's not surprising with the fatigue of ten centuries weighing down my poor carcass. But, as there is no remedy—'

The old Doctor gave a sign of assent.

'There is no real remedy. There should be a family law compelling the heir to the throne to choose a wife outside the fatal circle, from the aristocracy, the middle class, or the people, no matter where so long as the stock is sound. Such was the case in very remote times. Folklore tells us so. You remember the ballads and stories about the king's daughter either sitting at the window or asleep in the palace, waiting for a handsome knight to come and carry her off; and of the prince who loved Cinderella with the dainty little feet.'

The Prince had a vision of Marie's lovely, smiling face.

'Doctor,' he said, 'I am entirely with you. Try to convince my father, for I am already a convert. I am quite ready to get my marriage dissolved to try so tempting an experiment. Perhaps it would not take very long to find a Cinderella. Meanwhile—'

'Meanwhile, Your Highness, you must not overtax your strength. That is the only logical conclusion to our talk.'

'That is tantamount to not living at all,' answered the Prince, in a tone which impressed the old Doctor. 'You are very understanding, my old friend, yet you give me the same advice as all the rest. But the one impossible thing is to slow down the pace. If you could live a day with me. Listen a

minute and you will see. First let me give you another glass
of port. If you approve of it, I will send you a few bottles. I
don't think you will find better in Vienna.'

He filled the Doctor's glass and resumed:

'At half-past seven, Loschek wakes me. He doesn't find it
easy; probably I was not in bed until three AM, and I sleep
like a log in the mornings.'

'That's just where Æsculapius has a word to say,' interrupted the Doctor. 'Go to bed before midnight, and you will
be, if not all right, at any rate better.'

'Listen a moment, please; you will be able to form your
opinion presently. At half-past eight, the day's work begins
– business with my aide-de-camp, audiences, commissions
and so on. I am anxious to do my best. I have ideas; yes,
although I am a prince, I have ideas. I even have a plan!
Well, you see what happens! In my position one is not
allowed ideas; if one has ideas one is mistrusted. If one has a
plan the offence is even graver; one is immediately marked
down as dangerous. Dangerous, I, dangerous! Mark that,
Doctor! Throughout official circles I encounter obstinate
and concerted opposition. Oh! These gentry are very polite
and deferential. In theory they agree about everything, but
in practice they don't yield an inch. Nothing, nothing, nothing. That's the daily result of my infernal grind, and I have
given the best of myself to it for years. It's the same with
everything I touch. I am a Liberal, and therefore suspect.
Can't you imagine that it plays the devil with one's nerves?
Take your own case, as a doctor. Suppose, after infinite
trouble, you have found a remedy for a disease. You think
you can give relief to many poor devils. Very well; what
would you say if your colleagues were to combine unani-
mously against you and prevent your using it?'

'That does happen, sometimes, Your Highness, as a matter
of fact.'

'At any rate you get the satisfaction of curing those you do
treat. There you get tangible results. I get none. Yet my
patient is of some importance. It's the Dual Monarchy,

nothing less. These self-complacent gentlemen would let it collapse rather than try a single one of my suggestions. The knowledge of the gravity of the evils is beginning to tell on me.

'Now you know how I spend my day. When my work is finished I have only one idea – to forget everything, the irritation, the wasted time, and the fatuous people I have been struggling with. But that isn't all. There are State banquets and ceremonies to attend in the evening. One is always in the public eye – it's enough to drive one crazy. Sometimes at these dinners I feel I could murder everyone within reach. These people don't know that they owe their lives to the good champagne I am drinking.

'Then there are the everlasting intrigues. I am the hope of many good fellows, but there are always sharpers ready to feather their nests. Lastly, my old friend, not to mince matters, there are the women. We all know the story of the girls in a confectioner's shop being allowed to help themselves to sweetmeats, to make them lose their taste for them. In my position, alas, there is no forbidden fruit. I ought to feel disgust. I do, to some extent,' he hesitated a little, 'in my mind, if you understand me. But I have made a discovery. It is that women – how astonishing they are, and all so different that what one says of one is not true of another – that women *"versent aussi l'oubli"*, as the French song says. And, make no mistake, what I most need is forgetfulness. That is the end of my story.'

He threw himself back in his chair and closed his eyes. This long harangue had exhausted him. His face was drawn; there were pouches under his eyes; the veins stood out on his forehead. The Doctor looked at him uneasily.

A minute passed. Was he asleep? No, he sat up, looked at the Doctor for a moment, and continued as if he had not stopped:

'I have to forget who I am, just that; that I am one of a family which is, as you say, played out. I have to forget the injustice of my paying for the follies and excesses of twenty generations. Finally, I have to forget,' his voice was more serious, 'that I am not free, like the humblest of my subjects, to choose my own happiness. So, in the evening, after days such as I have just described, I do my best to forget. It is not easy to forget. It takes time. That is why I return at three or four in the morning to this old palace where all my ancestors are watching for me.'

As the result of Doctor Wiederhofer's visit, the Emperor decided that the Crown Prince should spend a fortnight at Abbazia on the Adriatic coast, with his wife and little daughter. They were to leave Vienna the day after Christmas.

CHAPTER III

ALARMS

WHEN MARIE HEARD the news – it was at about eight in the evening at the Hofburg, where she had been able to escape, while her mother and sister were at the opera – she burst into a flood of tears. Her Rudolph was going to leave her for a fortnight. Never had he been away so long. And he was going alone with the Princess. That the matter had been arranged by the Emperor in the hope of reconciling the Crown Prince and Princess, Marie did not doubt.

In vain the Prince tried to reassure her. He had been ordered away by his old friend Doctor Wiederhofer, who had urgently recommended a complete rest and a change of climate. He was only glad that the Doctor had not advised the French Riviera or Madeira. On an occasion of this kind he could hardly leave his wife in Vienna. But they would occupy two distinct suites in the hotel; she, her lady-in-waiting, her child and the governess would live in one; he and his aide-de-camp in the other. He would spend all his time yachting, and she hated the sea. And he was admiral of the fleet, moreover, which was stationed at Pola not far distant.

Marie refused to be consoled. The Prince took her in his arms, petted her and tried to make her laugh. He was so tender to her that, at last, he managed to soothe her. Never had he been so kind. Usually it was her, Marie's, mission to cheer him up and drive away his cares. This truly feminine vocation had always been a source of great happiness to her. Today the role was reversed. The hour he passed with her had a profound and lasting influence over the Prince. It brought to the surface a feeling that had been so completely dormant that he had been unaware of its existence. Seeing

Marie weep in his arms, quieting her grief and finally bringing back laughter to her lips filled him with an emotion he
had never previously experienced.

He could not express it to her that evening. He himself
did not yet grasp its full significance. He was obliged to leave
her early to go to the opera; but later in the evening the
matter kept recurring to him.

Generally he avoided any kind of introspection, knowing by experience that it brought nothing but bitterness and
disgust. Now all of a sudden Marie Vetsera had evoked a
different man, in whose companionship he found pleasure.
Where could he fortify this newly discovered personality
but in the presence of the magician at whose touch it had
come into being?

He yearned for Marie's society, and the obstacles in his
path added fuel to his desire. In her presence he was no
longer a cynic, and found that life still retained its zest and
value. The Prince who received Marie at the Hofburg with
impassioned ardour, but with all the reserve and scruples of
a sixteen-year-old lover, and with the trustfulness of a heart
which has never been betrayed, was one man. The Prince of
the Café Sacher and versed in court intrigues was another.
He saw this clearly now, and daily the conviction that he
could not exist without Marie took deeper root in him.

Everything is food for love. The Prince's conviction
gained strength rapidly. It found nourishment in Marie's
absence and presence alike. His disgust with his official
duties served to intensify the bliss of the rare hours he
spent with her.

One day, it was just after the middle of December, she was
with him in the little flower-laden salon at the Hofburg. He
loved her laughter and chatter, and often listened without
speaking. Marie, seeing his look of strain gradually disappear, was never in the least alarmed at these silences.
But that afternoon he seemed unnaturally quiet, and she felt
anxious without daring to say so.

The Prince, who was sitting on a cushion at her feet,

suddenly rose and began to pace the room. Absorbed in his thoughts, he appeared to have forgotten her. Suddenly he sat down beside her on the couch, put his arm round her waist and drew her toward him.

'Marie,' he said, 'I want to speak to you.'

His tone was so serious that she was frightened.

'I have been thinking for some time—'

Noticing her look of alarm, he whispered:

'There's nothing to be afraid of, my sweet. I love you so much that I can't live without you. That's all I wanted to say. Shall we make plans for our future?'

Marie could hardly believe her ears. Had he lost his head? Our future? Was there then a future for them? She had never thought that there could be.

'I don't understand,' she said and flung her arms round his neck. 'Our future?' she repeated. 'Do the words mean anything? But never mind! It's enough that your dear lips have uttered them. Our future. Say it again, I want to make quite sure there is no mistake.'

It was some time before he could speak. Marie danced about the room, threw him a kiss, brought him a flower. At last she came and settled in his arms, and said solemnly:

'I'm listening.'

The Prince explained rather confusedly that it was difficult to see far ahead, so involved was his position in the State and in his home. Contingencies might easily arise to alter the whole aspect of the situation. Merely discussing the main factors likely to affect his future was sufficient to renew his agitation. He spoke of his personal enemies, many of them in the highest places. On whom could he rely? There was no one. He was estranged even from the greater part of his family. They were as bigoted and reactionary as the rest.

'My father— We will speak of him another day. My mother, at the bottom of her heart, is very near me, but always avoids me. She often roams in this old palace, whose doors open at her approach. The other day I met her in one of the reception rooms. Taken unaware, she hastened her pace to make clear that she did not wish me to stop her. In passing, she gave me a little wave with her fan. Yet she loves me. Do you know of what she reminds me? A prisoner. The Hofburg, Vienna, the whole of Austria, is her prison. She doesn't breathe freely unless she is away from it all. She longs to escape and never come back. I am a prisoner, too, Marie—'

He stopped a moment, then, leaning toward her, whispered almost under his breath, as if afraid the walls might overhear:

'One day, I shall leave this country, and you will come with me.'

Marie heard this mysterious communication with astonishment. To leave the country! Naturally, at the slightest sign she would follow him. But how could he leave Vienna and Austria? The thing seemed impossible. Yet obviously he had something in view. She dared not believe it, but her heart beat fast at the idea that some day they might be united in the same destiny. Where? Little did that matter, provided they were together. She was dying to ask more about it, but, that afternoon, she dared not question him further.

On another occasion, in the Prater – he had just returned from Munich – he declared that he could not continue to live with his wife. Perhaps, in a fit of temper, she would carry out her oft-repeated threat to return to Belgium. In his heart, he thought it unlikely.

'She will never leave Vienna,' he said. 'The threat is one of her ways of exasperating me, that's all.'

But he himself had an audacious plan. He would entreat the Pope to dissolve his marriage on the plea that the Princess was unable to give an heir to the throne. His little daughter was five years old. The Princess had never had another child. That was a very strong argument, and the Pope would, no doubt, be influenced by his appeal. Here he became lost in a maze of political considerations, in which Marie followed him with difficulty. It was, however, clear that he had in mind a morganatic marriage with her. On other occasions he made no mention of the Pope. Another future was in store for them.

'When I am free,' he used to say, 'we will never separate. My *entourage* are firmly convinced that I am anxious for power. They are radically mistaken. How delighted they would be if they knew how utterly they have nauseated me. To be a free man, as my cousin Archduke John will be one day! To live our own life far from here! We must not think it's impossible. Perhaps, if we will it hard enough—'

One day, in discussing such matters with the feverishness which was now habitual to him, he stopped and began to laugh so strangely that Marie felt alarmed.

'Am I not stupid, darling,' he said, 'to worry so much? Is there not another way of renouncing the world and being together always?'

And as she looked at him with the intent of reading his innermost thoughts, he merely added rather mysteriously:

'Wherever I go, I know I can count on you to follow.'

Marie drew closer to him. Out of all this incoherent talk one thing was clear: whatever solution he contemplated she was always associated with it.

That was quite sufficient to keep her happy. She refused to weigh the chances and to follow the Prince in his calculations. In the midst of all the dangers surrounding her she clung desperately to one certainty: he loved her beyond everything, he never wanted to be parted from her.

At about that time they made an expedition to Schönbrunn. For long she had wished to see the Park in which he had played as a child. The public were not admitted. Neglecting for once his usual precautions, the Prince waited for her in Bratfisch's landau at the corner of the Marrokkanergasse, near the Salezianer Strasse. When Marie came out of the house with the Countess, she gave a hasty glance up and down the street. There was no one about, except two workmen slowly walking towards the Traumgasse, with their coat collars turned up. The Countess got into the landau with

Marie, and got out again at the first cabstand. Bratfisch
drove on to Schönbrunn. He stopped at a short distance
from the main gates. The Prince and Marie walked to the
park.

Just as they were going through the gates Marie looked
round. There was no one behind them, but, a hundred yards
or so away, she noticed two men loafing, in spite of the cold.
Their collars were turned up, and they at once reminded her
of the two workmen she had seen in the Salezianer Strasse.

'We are being followed,' she said hurriedly to the Prince.

To her amazement, he was not in the least concerned,
merely replying with a gesture of weary indifference:

'It can't be helped.' He didn't even turn round.

Marie was horror stricken. So the police knew of their
liaison. They must have been watched for a long time. Such
a thing had never occurred to her mind. Those two men
would make a report in Vienna. On what desk would it be
lying in the evening? Who would read it? To whom would it
be sent afterwards? To the Emperor, without doubt. She was
seized with a feeling of utter helplessness. All the occult
powers of the Empire seemed leagued against her. What
could she do against them? She would be smothered before
she could utter a cry.

Meanwhile the Prince noticed her silence and asked her
the reason. Not wishing to spoil an afternoon from which
they had expected so much pleasure, she gave him a smiling
reply. They were now walking along the deserted sidewalks
of the park.

'Where used you to play when you were a little boy?' she
asked.

The Prince laughed.

'There was not much time for playing. When I was quite
a small boy I was handed over to General Gondrecourt, who
introduced me to the charming severities of military discipline. And, you know, darling, however much, later in life,
one's soul protests against its preposterous tyrannies and
absurdities, one can never quite throw off the yolk. Today I

am a man; I have my own outlook on life, I have ideas a thousand miles apart from General Gondrecourt's. Yet after twenty years, he still retains a hold upon me. I can hear his metallic voice, and at the word of command I instinctively click my heels. There's no question about it, I am still under the yoke. It's a horrible thing. Could you love a soldier, Marie?'

She took his hand.

'You poor dear who had no childhood. It's my business to tease and amuse you now.'

It was beginning to get dark. They returned to Vienna. When she was alone, Marie gave way to her fears. How long would it be before the news was known and reached her mother's ears? Whichever way she looked, calamity seemed impending.

Meanwhile she had to part with the Prince, her only support. At the last moment, as a proof of his great love, he delayed for twenty-four hours his departure for Abbazia.

CHAPTER IV

THE IRON RING

TO HER OTHER fears a new one was now added. Would not the Princess use every means in her power to win back the Prince at Abbazia? Marie received tender letters from him. Was that enough to reassure her? She repeated to herself the Prince's words, in which he had promised to unite their destinies. These words, so noble and passionate at the time of their utterance, seemed to have lost all their ardour in the atmosphere of the Saleziander Strasse. They appeared lifeless, devoid of any inspiration. Nowhere could she turn for consolation. The Prince before leaving had warned her against the danger of taking the Countess any further into her confidence.

He returned in about a fortnight. After his absence he was more madly in love than ever. He had found the separation from her unbearable. Marie's presence gave fresh life, literally, to his feverish existence. Their relations had been pure hitherto, yet his craving was a physical one. Her merry chatter, her radiant laughter, her tender caresses brought to his jaded nerves a relief, the need of which he would always feel. At first, perhaps, he had thought of beguiling himself with her as with other women who had no illusions about the matter. But at their very first meeting he had recognized that Marie was of far finer mould. Ever since, he had kept faith with himself. Now he had vowed to make her his wife, whatever the obstacles might be.

Hardly arrived in Vienna, he had to leave for Prague. She saw him only in the distance at the opera. But, two days later, it was a Sunday, the Countess managed to smuggle Marie into the Hofburg at about seven in the evening.

She was at the end of her tether. She had made up her

mind to be always cheerful in his company and to conceal
her own troubles. But this time she had found the distress of
the separation too much. Directly she saw the Prince her
self-control gave way. She could not keep back her tears and,
throwing herself into his arms, she said:

'If I am always to be separated from you, I couldn't go on
living.'

The tone of her voice, the feeling that their love was
constantly menaced, the physical effect of her presence carried him away. He forgot the vows he had made. Marie,
delirious with joy at seeing him again, offered no resistance.

After the consummation of their love, the Prince realized
that he must not delay a moment in securing their future.
The time for words had passed. He threw himself headlong
into action.

That very night, on returning from the opera, he wrote a
private and confidential letter to the Pope, entreating him to
dissolve his marriage with the Princess. He adduced the inability of the Princess to provide an heir to the throne, and
their constant and increasing disagreement. He stated that
their relations had become so strained that they could no
longer endure each other's society, and a scandal was unavoidable – she would leave Vienna and return to Belgium.
He pointed out that such a state of affairs would bring
disastrous consequences to the house of Hapsburg, to the
State and to the Church.

The letter, although written in a moment of feverish excitement, was cleverly composed. The Prince despatched it
the following morning by a confidential messenger, instructing him to deliver it into the Pope's own hands.

On considering the matter more calmly, the Prince came
to the conclusion that his action had been over-rash. 'There
is not one chance in ten of my request being granted,' he
said to himself, 'but if the chance had been only one in a
thousand, I should have had to try it.'

He left on the following day for Budapest. The night before, he made a secret visit to his cousin, Archduke John

Salvator. They had not seen each other since the evening on which their relations had been so dramatically severed. The Prince had regretted the separation, as, although on many points he did not see eye to eye with his cousin, they agreed on matters of fundamental importance. On this occasion they conversed without any restraint, as if nothing had occurred to disturb their former intimacy. If political matters were broached, it was only because they shared the misfortune of their private lives being bound up with the existence of the State. The Archduke was shocked at the pallor and nervous state of his cousin, who showed every sign of being on the verge of a breakdown. An eavesdropper would have been surprised to hear the word death pronounced several times during the conversation. As the Prince was leaving, his cousin embraced him affectionately and said:

'It's only you who keep me here; if you were to disappear, you may be sure that I shouldn't remain a single day in this accursed country.'

On Saturday the 19th of January, the Prince returned from Buda in the morning. He had arranged for Marie to visit him at the Hofburg. As usual, she was accompanied by the Countess to the little postern gate, but she was rather surprised at Loschek taking her by an unaccustomed way.

'The Prince is giving audiences this morning,' the old servant informed her. 'He will see the Baroness in a salon next to the reception chamber.'

He ushered her into a vast salon, with Louis XV wainscoting in white and gold. Stiff-backed settees, covered with tapestry, and an antique desk stood on one side of the room, producing a formal effect. On the other side was another desk, of English make, a couch and two comfortable armchairs in leather. This side of the room was partly isolated from the other by a large screen which also concealed a little secret door in the woodwork.

The Prince was not there. Several minutes later Marie

heard his voice behind the large door on the right. Instinctively she retreated behind the screen. The door opened. The Prince ran over to her.

'I have a heavy morning's work, my love,' he said. 'Forgive me for bringing you in here. I was anxious to see you at once. I have one more delegation to receive; then I shall be free. Meanwhile, I have something for you here.'

He drew from his pocket a beautifully worked, polished iron ring and gave it to her.

'You know I have a weakness for inscriptions. Look inside.'

She read: '13th January 1889. I.L.V.B.I.D.T.'

'I understand the date, and I love it,' she said, giving him a rapturous look, 'but what do the letters mean?'

The Prince, speaking in a serious voice, deciphered them:

'In liebe vereint bis in dem tode.' (United by love unto death.)

Marie nestled closer against him. She could not speak. His words had conjured up a vision, and her eyes were fixed upon it. He had clothed death with strange beauty in uniting it to love. Was it death which would join them for eternity?

She raised her eyes to the Prince's.

'I will follow you where you will, my beloved.'

There was a gentle tapping at the door.

'It's Loschek,' said the Prince. 'Don't be alarmed.'

It was Loschek, who announced that the delegation was waiting.

'I shall not be long,' he said. 'I have only to make a few commonplace remarks to the good fellows in the next room. You will be quite safe in here; Loschek is on guard.'

He went out. Marie was left alone.

She felt as if separated from her normal personality. She had set foot for a moment in an unknown world, bathed in a serene atmosphere, far from earthly disturbances. The Prince's words had opened the gate. In that kingdom of eternal peace her troubles and anxieties had vanished.

She was sitting lost in her dream, when the sound of a

voice brought her back to reality. It came from the little door behind the screen. She heard the door open. A woman's voice said:

'Where were you, Loschek? I looked for you in His Highness's private sitting-room.'

Loschek replied in an embarrassed tone.

'I beg Your Majesty to pardon me. His Highness is receiving audiences this morning and ordered me to be in attendance here.'

Marie, still hidden by the screen, was trembling.

'How is His Highness since his return from Buda?'

This time the voice sounded nearer.

'His Highness is better, Your Majesty. He needs rest, no doubt; otherwise he is well.'

Marie, trembling all over, gathered that Loschek was doing his utmost to prevent the Empress from going any farther. Would he manage to keep her on the other side of the screen?

'Please tell him that I came to enquire about his health.'

'His Highness will be very touched by Your Majesty's solicitude.'

There was a slight pause. Marie was beginning to think that she had escaped, when the Empress resumed:

'I wish to write His Highness a note.'

With a few quick steps she went over to the little English desk. Then she noticed Marie blushing to the roots of her hair and not knowing which way to look. After a moment's hesitation she said, with exquisite courtliness:

'I beg you to excuse me for intruding.'

Next she turned towards Loschek, who looked the picture of confusion.

'You ought to have informed me that this young lady was here. You may leave us.'

Loschek withdrew.

The Empress looked at Marie again, who had by this time recovered her composure and was making a deep curtsy.

'I am anxious for news of the Prince,' she said. 'I will write him a few words, if you will allow me.'

She sat down at the desk, laid down her fan and found a pen and paper. She looked at Marie.

'Have you seen the Prince this morning?'

'Yes, Your Majesty,' replied Marie in a subdued voice and curtsying again.

'Did he look well? Please tell me.'

'I thought he looked a little tired.'

'Poor boy!' said the Empress rising and speaking to herself. 'The fates are undiscerning. He was not made for the life I gave him.'

Her voice, her stressing of certain words, and even her way of expressing herself reminded Marie so vividly of the Prince that her nervousness quite disappeared.

The Empress picked up her fan. She took several steps. Was she about to leave her thus? Marie now hoped that she would stay longer. She felt dimly that, in a hostile world, she had perhaps found an ally.

Meanwhile, after a slight hesitation, the Empress made up her mind. She went over to Marie and said:

'I have never had the pleasure of meeting you before. I do not go into society. Yet I know who you are. Our paths were unlikely to cross, but since chance has brought us together, I should like to speak to you for a moment. Please sit down.'

She pointed to a chair. She herself sat down on the couch. She played with her fan awhile, then with a swift movement she arranged the bottom of her long back dress. She looked at Marie again.

'You are even prettier than they told me. And how young you are! How old are you? I feel I can still ask you.'

'I am seventeen, Your Majesty.'

'Seventeen!' repeated the Empress. 'Can anyone really be seventeen?'

She paused, and, as if forgetting Marie again, added to herself:

'At seventeen I was already married, and already unhappy. Yet I was young, like you,' she looked at Marie again, 'and beautiful like you.'

Marie found courage to say:

'Your Majesty is still beautiful.'

'Like an old woman.'

She emphasized the words as if to seal a tomb in which her youth had long since been buried. There was another pause. Marie dared not raise her eyes. She heard the gentle tapping of the Empress's fan. She seemed to be following her thoughts. Then, in a changed tone, she said:

'I beg your pardon. I was dreaming, as a person does who has long lived alone. I must go. I do not wish my son to find us here together. I am glad to have seen you. Now I know that you are good and beautiful. I should like my son to be happy. He has so few years in which to be happy. Yet nothing else matters! It is more difficult for a prince than for others. I often pity him. I do not tell him so. Commiseration does no good. In this gloomy palace you look like a flower. You should not come back. Flowers fade quickly here. Come here and let me kiss you, my child. You are very close to my heart.'

She rose, took Marie in her arms and kissed her on the forehead. At last, very quickly, she left, holding her head high, her silk dress rustling behind her.

Marie, overcome with emotion, fell on the couch; with her head buried in her hands, she wept quietly.

Meanwhile the large double door opened, unnoticed by Marie, and the Prince appeared in the opening. He was saying his parting words to the delegation.

'Gentlemen, I thank you once more and bid you "Good day".'

The door closed behind him.

He entered the room and saw Marie lying on the sofa weeping like a child. He went over to her, caressed her and asked her the reason of her tears. She was soon comforted, but, still under the stress of her emotion, described the scene which had just taken place.

'I was so frightened that I couldn't utter a word. I was afraid quite without reason. At once, I understood that she at any rate did not wish to separate us. But there is something about her, I can't explain it, something grand and distant, mysterious, too, as if she knew things beyond our comprehension. She uses quite simple words, yet with a very deep meaning. Don't imagine that she tried to alarm me. On the contrary, she was very kind, even tender. Would you believe it? She kissed me. But she seemed to see farther than I can, and to pity me and us, as if terrible evils threatened us. She said nothing to make me think so; it was her manner, her way of looking at me and of being silent. I was so affected that, when she left, I could not help crying without any reason, you know, like the little silly I am. Still, Rudolph,' she continued, putting her arms round his neck, 'I am happy; there is only one real cause of unhappiness, separation from each other, but the ring you gave me just now reassures me.'

CHAPTER V

RUMOURS

RUMOURS BEGAN TO be bruited in society and court circles. 'The Prince,' said some, 'no longer confines himself to debauch. This time it is something else.' Knowing ones said that this 'something else' had been going on for a long time, and that the supper parties at the Café Sacher were merely a mask for hiding the real state of affairs. They expressed admiration of the Prince's skilful game and his elegant manner of putting the public off the scent.

What could this 'something else' be? Here rumour was divided. Some declared that a girl of quite marvellous beauty had taken by storm a man who, hitherto, had never lost his heart. Others wagged their heads in a superior way. Was it likely that a man like the Crown Prince would be content with a little white goose, however pretty? Would an exchange of looks at the opera and a clandestine meeting in the Prater (on the latter point rumour was very emphatic) appeal to a man who had tasted every pleasure? The suggestion that he had seen her at closer quarters could not be considered very seriously. The girl whose name was coupled with his had never been seen anywhere except with her mother or with Countess Larisch (at this name several people exchanged meaning looks, but for a very good reason restrained their tongues). The only reasonable conclusion was that the beautiful girl in question, to whose charms the Prince had admittedly succumbed, was herself a foil. For what purpose? Ah! there the keenest of them lost the scent. A well-known Polish woman of German origin was cited. A spy, without a shadow of doubt, or, if you preferred a less alarming label, an agent of the diabolical 'Iron Chancellor' who, displeased with the Prince's liberal ideas, wished to lead him back gently into the right path. According to another theory, a little *bourgeoise* had turned the Prince's head to such good purpose that, in comparison with her, the Empire and the Crown were but paltry baubles.

However it might be, all were agreed that this time the inconstant one was in deadly earnest. As for the consequences, which would ensue to the State, the Crown, the dynasty, political parties of every complexion, the Army and himself, so complex, so uncertain, so varying were they, that it was impossible to estimate them even approximately.

Meanwhile so many people mentioned the little Baroness Marie Vetsera by name that the rumours did not fail to reach the ears of the two people concerned. Count Hoyos, the Prince's staunch and disinterested friend, thought it his duty to put him on his guard. To his astonishment the Prince merely replied:

'Thanks, Hoyos. As a matter of fact I am in love with her. But I count on you to deny any rumour in which our names are coupled.'

As for Marie, she had the following experience. She had arrived at the opera one evening shortly before the curtain rose, and was walking along the corridor leading to the boxes, a few steps ahead of her mother and sister. At the half-open door of a box two ladies, friends of the Baroness Vetsera, were standing talking. Marie moved in their direction to exchange a few words with them. The ladies had their backs turned to her and were speaking with such animation that they did not hear her footsteps. Marie was now quite close to them. She heard her name and the Prince's mentioned. Directly the ladies noticed her, they stopped short in their conversation. Women of the world as they were, they could not hide a certain amount of confusion. Marie was tongue-tied. Fortunately the speedy arrival of Madame Vetsera put an end to the uncomfortable situation.

Had this incident occurred a month earlier, Marie would

have been considerably worried. That evening, it left her
almost indifferent. She felt herself the plaything of tremendous and mysterious forces, beyond her control, which would
hurl her, living or dead, she knew not where. What did it
matter whether or not people in Vienna spoke of her *liaison*
with the Prince? It would take time for the story to reach
her mother's ears, for the rumours lacked consistency. Time!
In those days she made plans only three days ahead. Who
could tell where she would be in a month or even in a
week?

The Prince was away once more for forty-eight hours.
That was what mattered. What news would he bring back?
Would there be a telegram from Rome? Her life hung on
this thread.

On his return from two days' hunting at his place at Orth
on the Danube, the anxiously awaited reply from the Pope
had not yet arrived.

There is no doubt that the above-mentioned rumours had
already determined the Prince to take extra precautions in
arranging his meetings with Marie. After certain innuen-
does made by the Princess, plainly showing that she was
aware of his *liaison*, he no longer dared to see Marie in the
Hofburg. He therefore asked the Countess to bring her to
the Prater in the evening. There could be no safer place than
the Prater at nine o'clock on a winter night.

In Bratfisch's landau, Marie was surprised to find the
Prince, if not cheerful, at least calm and able to speak on
any subject with complete detachment. He had wrapped her
in a fold of his cloak, and she snuggled blissfully in his arms.
He cared for nothing in the world but her. That night he
asked nothing more of life. He heeded neither thickening
rumour nor his wife's veiled threats. No reply from the Pope
had yet arrived. So be it! If the Pope refused his aid, he
would act without the Pope.

'As long as I am sure of you,' he said tenderly to Marie,
'nothing can really harm me.'

Darkness enfolded them. In the distance there was a faint glow from the lights of the hostile city. The frost rimmed the windows of the carriage, which, for a fleeting moment, held two beings oblivious of everything save the supreme joy of being together.

CHAPTER VI

EMPEROR AND SOLDIER

T W O D A Y S L A T E R, Saturday the twenty-sixth of January, was a red-letter day. They were to see each other in the morning at the Hofburg and to meet again in the evening at the ball given by the German Ambassador, Prince von Reuss. Marie was making her *début* that night. The Crown Prince and Princess were to be present. Marie had given the most careful thought to her *toilette*. She was to wear her mother's diamond crescent in her hair and, on her finger, the first of the rings given her by the Prince. She had told her mother that it was a present from their dear Countess Larisch on the occasion of her *début*.

But the fates willed otherwise.

The Prince, in the morning, was preoccupied, and, although he endeavoured to hide his despondency from Marie, she knew him too well not to notice it. He was still without news from Rome. Did that account for his depression? At any rate she set to work to dispel it, using a method she had often found successful. She began to speak of the happy days they would spend together in some secluded spot, far away from Austria, when the Prince had abdicated. There was for him no more alluring topic. For, even if the Pope granted a dissolution of his union, he would still be the Crown Prince, with the self-same round of duties, responsibilities and worries. In that case he certainly had hopes of obtaining his father's consent to his contracting a morganatic marriage with Marie. But would he succeed? Moreover, Marie was terrified at the idea. 'Living in full view of the public is fatal to real happiness,' she used to say, 'but how we should adore living quietly far away from the madding crowd!'

That morning she returned to this subject.

'You know,' she said, 'I believe you would soon tire of having nothing to do. You are not accustomed to it.'

'Twenty years' rest wouldn't be enough to get rid of all my fatigue. Where shall we go?'

They were soon launched into a discussion which carried them from Andalusia to the Basque country, from Algiers to Normandy, and from the South Sea Islands to Ceylon.

Marie brought it to an end by saying:

'After all, what does it matter? It will be Paradise wherever we are together.'

The Prince folded his arms around her.

'I have you tight in prison now!'

She brought the conversation back to a more matter-of-fact subject.

'Have you forgotten that long ago you promised to take me into the forest in winter? How can I trust a man who doesn't keep his promises?'

'I am going to shoot at Mayerling on Monday and Tuesday next,' he replied, 'in the heart of the Wiener Wald, in the foothills. I have a shooting box there. I would love to spend those two days with you. For the moment, it's impossible, alas!'

'How lovely that would be! But listen, Rudolph, if you take me there I shall not come back to Vienna.'

'Very well. That's understood. When we have made up our minds not to part again, I will take you there.'

At that moment Loschek's scratching noise was heard on the door. The Prince's mood changed in a trice.

'You see,' he complained, 'they won't give me a minute's peace. They are all in league against me. What have I done to them? Can't they leave me alone for a day?'

'Come in,' he called to Loschek.

The old servant entered.

'What is it now, Loschek?'

The Prince's voice betrayed his nervousness.

'One of His Majesty's aides-de-camp desires to speak to Your Highness.'

The Prince turned to Marie.

'Go into my room for a moment. It will be nothing important, but I shall have to see him.'

As soon as she had disappeared, Loschek ushered in the officer, who said that the Emperor desired to see the Prince without delay in his study.

Before the aide-de-camp had finished his sentence the Prince realized that his father had summoned him for the gravest of reasons and that the interview would decide his fate.

'I will follow you in a moment.'

The officer withdrew. The Prince fetched Marie back into the room. She noticed at once that he was upset.

'I have to go and see my father,' he said. 'He is always rather long-winded. I'm afraid I can't keep you, my love.'

Marie was frightened.

'Does he want to talk about me?'

'That is most unlikely. It's probably about some tiresome Army matter.'

She was not convinced.

'I'm afraid!'

He took her in his arms.

'Don't be alarmed, darling. You know that no one can separate us. If it comes to the worst, we will go to Mayerling together, even if we never return. I shall try to send you a line this afternoon. In any case, I shall let you know tonight at the ball how matters stand.'

They embraced passionately.

A few minutes later the Prince was introduced into the Emperor's study. It was a vast cheerless room, in which no piece of furniture ever changed its place. Chairs and armchairs were lined up like a picket of soldiers; no sheet of paper lay about on the desk or the table; no pen, no pencil but was in its appointed place. Two large windows with heavy green curtains hanging down stiffly as if made of sheet iron, let into the room the grey light of a bleak winter's day.

The Prince never felt at his ease there. In his state of mind that morning, with every reason to dread the impending interview, and fearing that he might be unequal to the struggle, his nervousness was at breaking-point. He visualized that cheerless study as a battlefield on which two adversaries were about to be locked in a death grip. With a presentiment of defeat in that strange encounter, he feared that his nerves would fail him. He did not know what weapons his father would choose. Never before had they discussed such questions. He could not imagine from what angle the Emperor would approach the matter. 'If only his manner would be official!' he thought to himself.

The Emperor was seated at his desk, in the undress uniform of a field-marshal. His few remaining hairs, his whiskers, his moustache were all perfectly white. Massive spectacles bridged his rather wide nose. He was reading with the closest attention a sheet of paper, following line after line carefully with his pencil. He motioned to his son to sit down and wait for a moment.

The Prince, while waiting, examined his father carefully, as if he had not seen him for a long time. In actual fact he had dined with him the previous evening.

'He has aged a lot,' he thought, 'and he's only sixty! I wonder if he ever was young! He's just an old bureaucrat in charge of the business of the firm Hapsburg and Co. He has his nose buried in red tape all day. He's just been looking through the record "Rudolph and Marie" and our lives are to be discussed on their merits exactly as if they were two strips of cloth for the uniforms of the troops.'

When the Emperor had finished reading his paper, he opened a drawer, arranged it carefully, laid his pencil on the desk in line with the other coloured pencils, removed his spectacles, wiped them with his handkerchief, put them back in their case and set it in its proper place between the writing pad and the pencils. Having done this, he turned to his son and began in a colourless voice:

'I received this morning from the Vatican a communication that greatly surprised me. I refer to a personal letter from the Holy Father. As it did not pass through the offices of the Curia, its contents are known only to His Holiness and to myself.'

'The official tone; I was sure of it,' thought the Prince, nerves already on edge. His father's monotonous voice caused him even greater irritation than the knowledge that at the appointed minute he would receive an answer of vital consequence to himself.

'I understand,' continued Franz Joseph, 'that on the fourteenth of January of this year you addressed a personal letter to the Holy Father on a matter of the gravest importance, without consulting me.'

The Emperor looked at his son in expectation of an answer. The Prince merely replied:

'It was about an entirely personal matter.'

'That is where you are profoundly mistaken,' continued the blank voice. 'Under no circumstances can such a matter be regarded as personal. It touches the highest interests of the State. The Holy Father has rightly judged it so, in addressing to myself the answer to your letter. A request such as you made can only emanate from me, the Emperor and head of the House of Hapsburg, invested, by virtue of the Covenant which determines this point, with supreme authority.'

The Emperor here indulged in several extremely learned comments on the legal niceties of the Covenant in which, in 1839, had been defined with profound wisdom the rights and prerogatives of the head of the family. With considerable skill he discussed the interesting problem whether the Emperor was bound by the Covenant or whether, as head of the family, he stood superior to it. And he seemed to invite the Prince to share his admiration for the foresight with which Ferdinand I and his advisers had drawn up the statute.

The Prince was raging inwardly. When the Emperor had at last finished he snapped out:

'But your answer, Father?'

The Emperor looked at him in amazement.

'Have you not drawn your conclusions? The answer is in the negative, my boy, in the negative.'

He nodded his head ponderously as if in approval of his statement, and again thought the moment opportune for voicing a few general considerations. The Prince was no longer paying attention.

Now that he knew the Pope's reply he saw that it could not possibly have been different. He had acted in a moment of despair. A man who sees two ways of escape tries both. If one leads nowhere he turns to the other. There remained the second, to go off with Marie. At that moment he hoped that his father would stop there for the day. The fight was only beginning, yet he felt overwhelmed with fatigue. He needed rest and time to prepare his flight.

But he had to hear his father out. The Emperor was under way and intended to develop his subject. 'My God, how slow he is,' thought the Prince. 'He's an old man.' He began to examine his father's ears. They had always seemed large. Had they grown larger? They reminded him of parchment. The blood seemed to have ceased circulating in them. 'They are dead,' he said to himself. 'I am sure they are going to drop off.' The idea tickled him.

The Emperor stopped. There was a pause. The Prince rose, as if the interview were over. His father signed to him to wait.

'I have not finished yet.'

He stroked his moustache, with him a sure sign of nervousness. 'The struggle is about to begin,' thought the Prince. He had a vision of Marie's laughing face, and felt full of fight.

'I have never had occasion to speak to you of your private life,' the Emperor's tone had changed a little, 'but today matters are at such a pitch that the Emperor and not the father intervenes. You have a *liaison*—'

The Prince could contain himself no longer. His patience

had been sorely tried. He forgot the respect due to his father and muttered brusquely:

'Am I unique in that?'

The Emperor, in a dry and authoritative voice, but without losing his calm manner, continued:

'You alone are under consideration now. You have not been able to keep your *liaison* secret. You have committed the gravest indiscretions. It has come to your wife's ears and you are well aware of the dangers in that quarter. To run risks of a scandal is out of the question for people in our position. We cannot afford one. But if the present course of events continues, an explosion is inevitable. An explosion would recoil upon our House.' In pronouncing that word, so pregnant with meaning to him, the Emperor raised his voice. 'We are encompassed by enemies. Too many busybodies have an interest in exploiting anything which might weaken the Monarchy. Do you wish by your wantonness to compromise the work to which our House has devoted its efforts for centuries?'

This was too much for the Prince. His father's tirade had galled him to the bone. How could he hear, unmoved, his eternal union with Marie qualified as a *liaison*? How could he bear the word wantonness applied to feelings which defied death? He was violently incensed, but by a tremendous effort he retained control of his temper. The Emperor, however, expected an answer.

'Have you nothing to say about the matter?'

'What do you wish me to do?'

'I wish you to break with Mademoiselle Vetsera.'

However much he may have expected this, the Prince winced. Her name seemed to resound through that vast silent room; the very furniture seemed to shiver. The Emperor remained stolid and impassive, his eyes fixed on his son. Choking with emotion the Prince could not utter a word. He shook his head emphatically.

The Emperor interposed:

'I think you don't quite understand.'

This time the Prince replied, beginning in a low voice which he raised as he proceeded:

'I was expecting this request. When you sent for me, I was perfectly aware of what you would say. To break with—'

He faltered. To use Marie's name in his father's presence seemed a sacrilege. Mademoiselle Vetsera? Was there a Mademoiselle Vetsera? He resumed:

'To break? That's impossible. Don't suppose that I say so in anger. For months I have been face to face with this question. And I have made a discovery. I have come to the conclusion that having only one life I wish to be – I hesitate to use the word, for it has probably never been uttered in this study – I wish to be happy.'

He stopped. His father appeared to scrutinize him curiously. 'He must think me the strangest of animals,' thought the Prince. He felt completely detached and continued without the least restraint in a tone he had never hitherto used to his father, in which a trace of impertinence was apparent.

'I am astonished that you compel me to decide for myself. With your considerable wisdom and experience, I imagined that you would leave me to find a mode of life that would reconcile two conflicting things, my duty toward you and my duty toward myself. Is it really impossible?'

The Emperor shook his head. He kept tapping the table with his paper knife. It was the only sign of nervousness he showed. The incessant noise of the tapping irritated the Prince, making him feel he had not gained an inch of ground. Suddenly he decided to attack.

'I have no desire for power; the atmosphere in official circles is vitiated. For a long time I thought I might be useful. Your advisers have dispelled that illusion.'

'There are no advisers,' said the Emperor. 'There is only myself.'

'That matters little. Despite all my work, despite my numerous duties, I feel I am useless in the Empire. I have ceased to have any faith in what I am doing. My role is purely ornamental. I therefore renounce it. There is no law to prevent me, as far as I am aware.'

The paper knife came down with a crack on the desk.

'What is this I hear?' said the Emperor, hoarse with anger. 'You forget you have a duty to fulfil—'

The Prince did not allow him to finish.

'Another will fulfil it. Will this be the first time in the history of our House for the succession to pass to a collateral branch? My cousin Franz-Ferdinand would take my place and would occupy the position exceedingly well. His ideas are perfectly safe, whereas I am mistrusted all round. Your counsellors would be delighted to see my back.'

'You shall not go.'

The Emperor's voice came trenchant, like an axe. The Prince flushed scarlet, but he made yet another effort to control his temper.

'I might not have been born,' he argued. 'I may die to-morrow. In that case the Monarchy would continue. In my cousins you have an inexhaustible reserve.'

'Enough of these sophistries,' said the Emperor.

'But they are not sophistries,' snapped the Prince. 'Have you not discovered that during the last hour? I have found happiness, at last. I do not intend to forego it. If you will not allow me to enjoy it in my public capacity, I shall retire to private life.'

'And on what will you live?'

The question came point-blank and stopped the Prince. He looked at his father with fury.

'Do you mean that you would deprive me of the means of existence? That is, no doubt, in your power, but it would be an abominable thing.'

'Silence! I am not here to answer your questions. I shall act for the best.'

'Be careful. There is another way out of the difficulties you are placing in my path.'

A long pause followed the threat contained in this sentence. Franz-Joseph put his elbows on his desk, and, with a gesture familiar with him when needing time to reflect, buried his head in his hands.

The Prince rose, and, heedless of etiquette, strode up and down the room. His mind was made up. He would obtain his liberty; if not— The idea of giving up Marie never even crossed his mind. They would go together, whatever fate might be in store for them. Their union would never be broken. The Prince felt so weary that his soul craved for peace. Why should he not leave then and there the tortures of that frigid room? What did he still hope for? It seemed absurd to go on struggling when there is a place of easy access, a place where there is no strife, the land of eternal peace. He had of that enchanting region a vision so alluring, so serene, that he kept it to the end of that painful inter-view.

At last the Emperor sat up erect. He went over to his son and, placing his hand on his shoulder, drew him over to a couch.

'Let us sit down. It is no longer the Emperor speaking. Let us talk as father and son.'

This was a new and totally unexpected attitude. The Prince did not unbend. It was, without doubt, a manoeuvre of his father, an old and skilled hand in the art of managing men. He decided to listen carefully and take no risks. He responded to the invitation with an eagerness that seemed genuine to the Emperor.

'Nothing could give me more pleasure.'

The Emperor made him sit down beside him.

'You are my son, my only son,' he began. 'I love you, but for some reason or other we have never had occasion to open our hearts to each other, as father and son should. I have no time to myself, as you know.' He sighed. 'What a crushing load my shoulders have to carry.'

He continued in a kindly tone, speaking of his life since he had come to the throne at the age of eighteen, in the height of the storm raging across Europe and bowling over dynasties like houses of cards. He spoke of forty years of incessant and thankless labour, beginning daily at cock-crow, of old age upon him with never a day of rest.

He spoke gently, without complaining, without lauding himself; and these newly revealed traits of his father's character gave the Prince a different impression of him. 'How clever he is,' he said to himself, 'far more clever than I suspected.' The saying of a writer of that day came to his mind, a saying which had astonished him and which he had not understood before, 'The Hapsburgs are born artists.' Now it dawned on him that his father had talent! At that moment he admired him, but the fact in no way affected his decision.

The Emperor rambled on:

'We represent, my boy, a time-honoured dynasty. In the opposition circles frequented by you – I bear no ill-will,' he hastened to add, 'to hear the opposite side is part of your role as heir apparent – they have, I know, rather a poor opinion of my policy. Those who are not in power think only of the present. I, who am only a link in a chain of men, am obliged to think of the generations that come after us. My people do not always understand the wherefore of my actions, but I have gained their confidence because they feel dimly that their Emperor and King works disinterestedly for them. If we deserted our posts, my boy, if the dynasty disappeared, the people of our Empire, united today, would break out into fratricidal strife. In place of a great and prosperous Empire, forged piece by piece by your ancestors, there would remain nothing but a few feeble states, menaced by powerful neighbours, fearful of the morrow. You know well, Rudolph, that it is impossible to gainsay what I am saying.'

At other times, the Prince would have seized with enthusiasm that, his first, opportunity of broaching a political discussion with the Emperor. Today it was too late; the issue at stake was no longer the welfare of the Empire, but the happiness of Marie and himself. His discomfort increased as he found himself at closer grips with a cunning adversary who knew how to choose his ground. He would be defeated without fail. When the moment was opportune, he must break off. Still, out of weakness, he temporized.

'Perhaps it is a mistake to work for the future. Nations are never satisfied, they don't know the meaning of gratitude. Again, a hurricane may burst upon us from the north. Is our ancient dynasty built to endure?'

'I do not know,' said the Emperor, 'and sometimes I doubt it. Perhaps I shall be the last Emperor. But our duty stands. A soldier does not discuss the word of command. Soon it will be your turn to take charge. I count on you.'

The Prince, almost in a whisper, as if speaking to himself said:

'The only thing that matters is that the post is not abandoned. If a soldier is reported missing, there must be another to fill his place.'

The Emperor quivered. Was it his son, a Hapsburg, speaking? They sat there close to each other, yet an abyss yawned between them. He remained motionless, his mind a blank, not knowing which way to turn.

At that moment, an unexpected incident occurred. The clear notes of the bugles rang out, sounding the relief of the guard. During the forty years of his reign the Emperor had never failed to watch the relieving battalion march by the Palace at that hour. Whatever work he was engaged in he left, went over to the window, and his soldier's heart warmed at the sight of his fine soldiers training for the defence of the Empire.

That day, as on every preceding day, the call of the bugles brought him to the window. Mechanically the Prince followed him. For a while the hostile atmosphere of the room was dispersed by the joyous strains of martial music. They were just two men watching with keen eyes a spectacle in the details of which they were specialists.

'The regiment of riflemen from the Tyrol,' said the Emperor. 'How splendidly they swing by.'

'The men come from Meran and Innsbruck,' commented he Prince. 'Hardy fellows, and they never grumble.'

'Our new regulations for the instruction of recruits are giving excellent results. Some of these men have had only six months' service. The progress they have made is marvellous.'

They chatted, as men do, who have worn a uniform all heir lives. For the time being, their disagreements had disappeared. Suddenly, the Emperor took his son's arm.

'You are a soldier; I am a soldier too. On this ground we can talk. Look at those fellows. They are young; they have heir whole lives before them. They do not know me; they expect nothing from me. I mean little to them but hard work and iron discipline. Very well, if tomorrow trouble arose, or if a hurricane from the north, as you suggested just now, burst upon us, if I had need of them, they would answer my call, aye, every man of them, and they would shed their last drop of blood for me! Have you thought of that? And you my boy—'

During this harangue, the Prince's exasperation was at boiling pitch. The Emperor was playing, with the skill of a consummate artist, on his most responsive feelings. There seemed something disloyal in his using such a weapon. It almost seemed as though, at a prearranged moment, he had produced a military band to throw into relief the pathetic side of his argument, just as, in melodramas, the orchestra plays on the emotions of the audience in a sensational situation. 'I am not going to be caught,' he thought. 'How can I escape?' He had ceased to listen. He kept repeating to himself the words his father had just used: 'I shall act for the best.'

That was a stock phrase of the Emperor, used for deferring a request he had decided to refuse. They had chaffed him about it in the family when circumstances had been propitious. It had, therefore, a definite meaning. The Emperor, who had personal control of the entire wealth and appanages of the House of Hapsburg, would not give him a cent if he left Austria. 'I shall act for the best' was a kind of blackmail to induce him to break with Marie, a blackmail of a particularly absurd kind, for their two lives were one and indivisible. The Emperor, with his crass stupidity and blunted feelings, would understand that later, when he saw them die together. For the moment, despite the anger that consumed him, the Prince's brain was as cold as ice. He would have to be diplomatic, for his father would not let him leave until he had given him a promise. Of what value was a promise extracted by such methods? That was a matter for his own conscience to decide. But even under the pressure of dire necessity, he was unwilling to perjure himself directly. He must find a way of giving a non-committal answer. It was a question of words. Who was responsible? The purblind Emperor, of course. Until the end of the interview the Prince manoeuvred for the right to die, with as much *sang-froid*, courage, and skill, as another man uses in defending his right to live.

These considerations flooded his brain while his father was speaking. The Emperor finished with another of his favourite aphorisms:

'So we are agreed.'

'There remains only one point to clear up,' said the Prince, deliberately adopting his father's tone. 'I should like to see Mademoiselle Vetsera once more. There is something unnecessarily cruel in sending her away as one dismisses a Minister.'

The Emperor's face lit up with pleasure; he was almost smiling. He was, in fact, distinctly proud of his elegant manner of getting rid of a Minister who had lost his favour. The former, after a gratifying audience, believed himself in the highest favour, only to find, on returning to his house, a letter of resignation ready for his signature.

'I have no objection to your seeing her once.'

'Alone,' the Prince stipulated.

'Alone, if you wish it, although these final interviews are extremely painful. It is always advisable to avoid them.'

The Prince was beside himself with rage at his father's words.

'That is my business,' he growled.

'Very well, as you like. But please let it be for the last time. I would like your word of honour.'

'I give it you.'

The Emperor rose. He was minded to embrace his son. But the Prince's face was drawn and haggard, and in his eyes glittered a burning light. Franz-Joseph merely sighed and concluded on the official note:

'That is all I have to say.'

CHAPTER VII

MAYERLING

THE BALL GIVEN on Saturday the 26th of January by Prince Henry of Reuss at the German Embassy was the most brilliant event of the season.

The Crown Prince and Princess Stephanie were present. The Embassy was filled to overflowing with the *élite* of the gayest society on earth; Archdukes and Archduchesses, the diplomatic corps, courtiers, statesmen, the chiefs of the Army and the matchless beauties of the Dual Monarchy. Dazzling *toilettes*, glittering uniforms, ancestral coronets, tiaras, orders, necklaces, pendants, diamonds, pearls, sapphires and brilliants, gleamed and sparkled under the rays of crystal chandeliers. Dainty waltz music floated from Johann Strauss's band. It was a moment of luxury and pleasure, of forgetfulness and reprieve in this ruthless struggle for existence, one sweet smile breaking through gloom – a ball!

Who would believe that over the heads of two of the guests hung the sentence of death? They had barely three days to live. Yet, they had come to the ball. One was the highest personage of the assemblage, His Imperial and Royal Highness the Crown Prince Rudolph; the other, the loveliest, the most charming, and the youngest of all these beautiful women – she was only seventeen – Baroness Marie Vetsera, who that evening was making her *début*. She was dressed in pale blue, she wore a diamond brooch, a crescent in her hair, and on her finger a sapphire ring. Ten men, titled and wealthy, were in love with her, but she had betrothed herself secretly to death.

The Prince was in a gay mood tonight. He moved, gallant and smiling, through the crowded salons. Presently he exchanged a few words with Maria Vetsera. Prying eyes were

ixed on them, on account of the wild stories afoot, you know
- can one believe a word of them? Look at his easy assur-
ance! Look at her graceful bearing! After the customary
compliments, in which the Prince excelled, one heard: 'We
are to shoot at Mayerling, on Monday and Tuesday.' That,
and nothing more. Decidedly there was nothing in it. They
chatted for a minute, then separated and were lost in the
moving crowds. Where would their next meeting be?

Was it possible to remain so light-hearted and unconcerned when death was drawing near? Surely they were
unaware of its approach. That was the simple reason of his
frank gaiety, of the happiness shining in her clear young
eyes.

No, they were not unaware. They had themselves written
their fates on the scroll of destiny. They were to die together. The morning's interview with the Emperor had
settled it. Marie had learned the decision, a few hours since,
in a note from the Prince, full of tenderness and love, almost joyful at the thought of escaping from a world that
tortured them. For the moment, she thought only of one
thing, that she was to live alone with him, for a day or two,
far from the public gaze. The knowledge of that was enough
to light up her young face. This evening she knew that she
pleased him, that he longed to hold her in his arms. Surely
no ball could be more wonderful than this. She danced with
Count Hoyos; she had always liked him for his friendship
with the Prince. And she danced with Miguel of Braganza.
He was a cousin of the Prince. He, too, was in love with her;
he would marry her tomorrow if she would accept his hand.
To refuse so princely a match, what elegance! She was viva-
cious tonight, he liked her thus.

There was a lull in the dancing. What was it? It was the
Crown Princess moving round the salons on the arm of the
German Ambassador. As she passed, the men bowed low,
the women curtsied to the ground.

Marie and Miguel of Braganza stood aside to let them
pass. The Princess moved on, bowing on every side. She was

tall and stout, and had lost her figure since the birth of her
only child. Marie watched her coming. The Princess seemed
to her devoid of beauty, of tenderness and of grace; she had
reduced to despair a prince whose equal Austria had not
known, the hope and joy of the peoples of the Dual Monarchy; it was she who had condemned him to death. These
thoughts whirled through Marie's brain, filling her with
anger. The Princess was only three paces away. She stared at
Marie with curiosity, with defiance. How can Marie suffer
the insolence of that look? Many a pair of eyes was watching
the encounter of the Princess and the girl who was said to
be her rival. She was only one pace away. The women near
Marie curtsied, the men bowed. The Princess eyed her up
and down. Marie stood rigid. Her knees did not bend as
etiquette required. Head erect, she threw back the challenge
with her stare. The Princess and the Ambassador had
passed. A rumour ran round the room from group to group,
was whispered from ear to ear, passed from guest to guest,
under the crystal chandeliers, on the tapestried seats, to the
joyous strains of the band, between two glasses of champagne.

Two days later. It was the dusk of a winter's day. Clouds
were scudding over a storm-racked sky, and pink streaks of
light appeared in the west over the mountains; the branches
of the fir trees were laden with half-melted snow. A cluster
of small buildings surrounded by a wall squatted on the hill-
side; from there the view extended over a valley with several
houses grouped round a steepled church. This was Mayerling, the Prince's shooting lodge, about forty kilometres from
Vienna.

The Prince and Marie followed a path winding through
the forest. He had his arm linked in hers, a living represen-
tation of the truth, for, if he showed the way, yet it was he
who leaned on her. The profound stillness was untroubled
save by the tapping of a woodpecker or its cry as they

approached. The path rose steeply. At times, she stopped to rest.

'I am out of breath,' she said, taking his hand and placing it on her heart.

The Prince could feel its rapid beating through her sable coat. How strongly the rich young blood coursed through her veins!

'I should love to lose myself, Rudolph, but with you here it's impossible. You know each one of these trees, and they watch over us. So I cannot be afraid.'

They climbed higher. They knew there was no necessity for speech. Having nothing to hide, they did not fear each other's silence. Marie was at one with the winter forest which she had known so long in her dreams.

It was time to return, night was upon them. In the distance, two or three lights winked in the village. A few more steps brought them to the lodge.

A large room served as salon and dining-room; trophies of the chase and hunting pictures decorated its walls. And what wonderful flowers! Marie had never been so fêted. Was she not like one of those rosebuds that would die so soon? The Prince drew a curtain; behind it was the minute sleeping chamber; a vast bed almost filled it; at the back there was a dressing-room.

'That is all,' he said. 'Can you manage?'

She buried her face in his shoulder to hide her blushes.

Marie had left home in the morning with nothing but a handbag, as if she were going shopping. In the dressing-room, however, she found night things, a lovely tea gown of white voile and lace, and dainty swansdown slippers. The Prince had thought of everything. She kissed him again because he had desired that she should appear beautiful at dinner.

This dinner, which was attended by Rudolph's two friends, Prince Philip of Coburg and Count Hoyos, would have frightened her on another occasion. But she and Rudolph were already far from the world, in a secluded spot where all forms of etiquette were forgotten. She still continued to chat to the Prince as her lover. How was it that, hearing her talk away like that, they did not understand that they both were in the face of death? They said nothing, surely this was odd? They were a merry party during dinner. Bratfisch was summoned to whistle popular airs to them. He was so extraordinarily funny that Marie laughed heartily.

All retired to rest in good time, for the Prince and his friends expected to make an early start in the morning. Unfortunately the weather had suddenly changed; a wild storm howled and raged outside. It was more than doubtful whether there would be sport on the morrow.

For the first time, Marie knew the exquisite joy of sleeping in her lover's arms. She awakened late and found him at her side. So he had not been able to go shooting.

He would not leave her for a moment. Outside, snow and rain squalls lashed the moaning trees. But his mood was merry and bantering. How she loved to see him so care-free and happy.

After luncheon, a lull in the storm provided an opportunity for a short walk in the forest. The Prince was composed and serene. The past had had its terrors for him; now his eyes, like hers, were turned toward the future. She thought of all he was giving up out of love for her. One day she had seen in the treasure chamber the crown of Charlemagne, of solid gold and studded with precious stones. She pictured the crown on his beloved head. 'How splendid he would look. And for my sake—' She did not think once of the sacrifice of her own divine youth, or of the grim terrors of the last hour, so near at hand. She rejoiced at the thought of accompanying him there where he had chosen to go. Could she let him go forth alone on that journey from which there is no return? And he, in the presence of his beloved, was supremely happy.

The darkness was gathering fast. She feared the night air for him. They hastened back to the lodge. Lamps were fetched.

'I have a letter to write,' he announced.

She looked at him anxiously. Had he still business to transact? Did he still cling to life?

He read her thoughts and explained:

'It is to my mother. There is a cemetery near by in the woods, at Alland. I am asking her to have us laid there side by side, that those who suffer from a thwarted love may bring flowers to our grave and pray. Flowers will grow on it, and in our sleep we shall hear the soft whisperings of lovers.'

Marie wrote letters to her mother, her sister and her brother. She begged them to forgive her for leaving them thus. She and the Prince belonged to each other; in this world peace was denied them. She asked her brother not to grieve and promised to keep watch over him from the other world.

At dinner, only Count Hoyos was present. Prince Philip had returned to Vienna and was to take a note to the Emperor, begging him to excuse the Prince from the family dinner party at which he was expected.

Now night had fallen. Silent, or exchanging words of love, they remained for long interlaced in each other's arms. At last, nestling against him, she sank into a peaceful sleep, whispering the last words she would ever utter:

'Oh, if I could sleep on for ever.'

She fell asleep with the print of kisses on her half-closed lips.

She slept on, trustful as a child. Night enfolded them in its black mantle. She did not hear a sound of stifled moaning. Nor, at the first pale glimmer of dawn, did she hear a drawer softly open, a click— She did not see the King of Terrors gliding towards her like a wolf in the dark.

The first shot from the Prince's revolver woke Loschek, who slept near his master's room. Only half awake, he did not guess where the report had come from. One of the keepers, of course. Still, he felt anxious. As he arrived in the hall outside the Prince's room, a second shot rang out. This time he had no doubt. The report came from the Prince's room. He rushed to the door. It was bolted on the inside. He rushed to fetch Count Hoyos. Between them they burst open the door.

On the bed lay Marie Vetsera, covered with roses. Death had struck her down as she slept. Across the bed lay the body of Rudolph, *ci-devant* Crown Prince of Austria and Hungary, his skull horribly shattered by a revolver bullet through the right temple.

EPILOGUE

THE SAME MORNING, shortly after eleven o'clock, Madame Schratt arrived at the Empress's apartments. She was, as usual, sprightly and cheerful. An intimate conversation began at once between these two women, of such very different characters, who shared the Emperor's confidence. Madame Schratt was able to take the Empress out of herself, too.

Just after her arrival the door of the salon opened, and Madame de Ferenczi, the Empress's favourite lady-in-waiting, entered. She showed signs of being upset; but the Empress, pointing her finger at her, said laughingly to Madame Schratt:

'Look, she dramatizes everything. I am sure she is just going to tell me that one of my furs is moth-eaten.'

This sally was far from producing the expected effect on Madame de Ferenczi who, with a letter in her hand, drew nearer to the Empress. The latter, on looking at her more closely, was seized with alarm.

'What is it? Tell me quickly.'

Madame de Ferenczi endeavoured to speak, in vain. The Empress, now thoroughly frightened, seized her by the shoulders and stared at her in dumb amazement, as if to read her thoughts. The wretched lady-in-waiting, trembling like an aspen leaf, at last managed to stammer out:

'Count Hoyos has just arrived from Mayerling—'

She could get no further. And, feeling the Empress's eyes devouring her, she added in a faint voice:

'A fearful tragedy! The Crown Prince is dead!'

The Empress swayed beneath the blow. Madame Schratt rushed to support her. She and Madame de Ferenczi applied restoratives. The Empress's indomitable spirit asserted itself. With the tears still streaming down her face, broken voiced, she asked for details. Was it suicide? She thought of the end of so many of her own people and shuddered. The Prince had taken with him young Baroness Vetsera. She took the letter from Madame de Ferenczi and read the first words: 'Mother, I have killed—' She could read no more. Without uttering a word, with her head in her hands, she sobbed her heart out. A moment later, she straightened herself.

'The Emperor, he must know at once—'

Then, turning to Madame Schratt:

'Which of us will break the news to him?'

The two women looked at each other. Which of them should it be?

They remained there, stricken and faltering. At that moment they heard footsteps on the four stairs leading from the Emperor's apartments.

'It is he,' murmured the Empress. She drew closer to Madame Schratt.

The door opened. The Emperor came in. His wrinkled face showed the look of relief seen on a schoolboy's face on escaping for a few minutes from his class.

The Empress went up to him resolutely and, very gently, but without keeping anything back, in a few words told him the awful news.

For a moment the Emperor seemed not to understand. He looked from the Empress to Madame Schratt in blank amazement. Then, as if felled by a blow, he collapsed on a couch.

For long the two women sat beside him, each mutely caressing a hand. He made no attempt to struggle against his terrible grief. The blow had smitten him as a father, as a believer, and as Emperor. His son's words in the scene on the previous Saturday rang persistently in his ears: 'There is another way out of the difficulties you are placing in my path.'

He had not believed that the threat meant anything. That

is the kind of thing people say but never carry out. Now he remembered the pallor of his son's face and the fever burning in his eyes. He had acted for the best as he had said. But events had proved too strong for him. Suicide! That his son, his only son, his only hope should kill himself! It was monstrous, incredible, staggering. And the Church! What would the Church's attitude be? Must his son go before the Supreme Judge without absolution? Must he pay for a moment of aberration with everlasting punishment? And the Monarchy, the fruits of the patient labours of his ancestors during centuries, would it survive the blow? Whichever way he turned, he saw disaster imminent. The minutes passed without his stirring. Yet decisions were urgently needed. Count Hoyos was waiting in his study. Rudolph's body lay yonder, still with the girl's. He removed the tear stains from his cheeks, embraced the Empress and Madame Schratt and made his way to his apartments.

Orders began to be issued from the Hofburg. Count Taafe, the Emperor's right-hand man, summoned from the Reichrath, arrived at half-past one. The prefect of police and other members of the civil authority were already present. Amid the general consternation measures were hurriedly taken.

Count Szecsen von Temerin, a senior police officer, one of the Emperor's doctors, Professor Wiederhofer, and various officials of the court left forthwith for Mayerling with orders to bring back the Prince's body. As regards Marie Vetsera, instructions unutterably heartless.

The party sent to Mayerling was back at the Hofburg by a quarter past one in the morning. The Crown Prince was laid in his apartment overlooking the Schweitzerhof. No notice had been taken of his wish, expressed in his letter to the Empress, to be buried side by side with Marie in the little cemetery at Alland. In the eyes of the Hofburg, Marie did not exist and had never existed.

The Prince lay on a camp bed; the room was full of flowers; a red silk sheet covered his body; his head was bound with white linen, which concealed the gaping wounds made by the bullet.

The impression made by the news of their beloved Prince's death on the people of Vienna is indescribable. The main streets of the city were packed to overflowing with excited people demanding details of the calamity. In places the crowds got beyond control of the police, and the troops had to be called out. Several civilians were severely wounded; one was killed. It seems that Destiny exacts a toll of human life for the birth and death of the exalted. Once again this strange inexorable law declared itself. The first official version stated that death was due to the rupture of an aneurism of the heart.

During the night the post-mortem examination was held. In spite of elaborate precautions, the truth began to leak out. The doctors' report appeared on Friday, the first of February, their verdict being suicide owing to temporary mental aberration.

The fact of suicide having been established, the Emperor despatched a telegram of two thousand words to the Pope, requesting a Christian burial for his son. It was a matter that deeply affected not only himself but those nearest and dearest to him. The Vatican remained obdurate. How could the fact of so flagrant a case of suicide be concealed? The Emperor telegraphed again. If the Church should deny the final consolation, he had decided to abdicate. Finally, in spite of Cardinal Rampolla's opposition, Pope Leo XIII was moved by the Emperor's appeal and conceded the privilege of a Christian burial in compliance with the rites of the Church.[1] The funeral took place on the fifth of February

---

[1] Franz-Joseph had considerable reason for his fears. He was accurately informed of the part played in the matter by Cardinal Rampolla. Thirteen years later, at the conclave following the death of Pope Leo XIII, the Cardinal paid dearly for his scrupulous fidelity to the canons of the Church. When it seemed certain that he would be elected as Pope by a large majority, Austria exercised an ancient privilege of exclusion against him. Franz-Joseph had not forgotten.

at four o'clock, the Crown Prince's body being brought to the Capuchin church, where all the Hapsburgs and one of their kinsmen, the Duke of Reichstadt, lie buried.[1]

Neither the Empress nor the Crown Princess nor the Archduchesses was present. They attended a special service held in the Castle chapel. The Emperor was very composed. On his arrival at the church he glanced round the Assembly to satisfy himself that the prescribed arrangements had been duly carried out. During the Mass he remained motionless. He gave way only for a moment later, in the crypt, when the coffin was opened for the handing over of the Prince's remains to the Prior of the Order by the Grand Marshal of the Court, Prince Hohenlohe, who asked the customary question:

'Do you recognize the mortal remains of Rudolph, Archduke of Austria, and, in his life-time, heir apparent to the throne?'

The Prior replied with the traditional sentence:

'Yes, I recognize them and, henceforth, we will keep pious watch over them.'

Let us quit the crypt where so many exalted personages were assembled round the tomb of a prince whom Love has brought to the grave; let us leave the purple hangings emblazoned with the Imperial arms drooping on the cold damp walls; let us leave the wandering souls in this vault to give themselves over to grief and salute the wretched victim who has arrived amongst them still all bespattered with fresh young blood: let us turn to Marie Vetsera utterly forsaken in the spot where she was killed. No words can describe the callous cruelty with which the remains of the charming girl were treated.

---

[1] This was the last ceremony at which Archduke John Salvator appeared. A few months later he renounced his titles and rights. He married Milli Stubel, took the name of Jean Orth, and left Austria. In June 1890 the schooner *Santa-Maria*, which he had bought and in which he had left for the Southern Seas, was lost with all hands near Cape Tres Puntas.

On Monday 28th of January, after Marie had left Vienna forever, Countess Larisch-Wallersee returned alone to the Salezianer Strasse. In breaking the news of Marie's disappearance, she feigned distraction, and told the Baroness Vetsera that Marie had slipped away from the carriage while she had gone into a shop for a moment. She added that some time previously Marie had written a note threatening to throw herself into the Danube.

The Baroness's stupefaction, terror, and grief at this astounding story may be imagined. The Countess next attempted to reassure her friend, but merely succeeded in torturing her in another way by blurting out:

'Marie has no intention of committing suicide. She is madly in love with the Crown Prince and has gone off with him.'

'But she doesn't even know him,' exclaimed Madame Vetsera.

Upon this, Madame Larisch-Wallersee, being careful not to say a word of her own leading part in the intrigue, related the whole story of Marie's *liaison* with the Crown Prince.

Madame Vetsera could not believe her ears. Her daughter, who was hardly ever out of her sight, the merest child, the mistress of the Crown Prince! At any cost she must find her at once. She proposed to go without losing a minute to see Count Taafe, the Prime Minister, who was a personal friend. The Countess dissuaded her. The Count was inclined to be garrulous; the story would get about. She offered instead to go and see the prefect of police; she kept repeating: 'I lost Marie, I must find her again.'

She did go to see the prefect of police, accompanied, at Madame Vetsera's request, by her brother Alexander Baltazzi. The visit, however, proved fruitless. There was little that the prefect could do. He was emphatic on two points: first, that he could not set the police in motion at all without a formal complaint lodged personally by the girl's mother; second, that it was against the law of the land for the police to take action of any kind against the Crown Prince.

In any case the Baroness was reluctant to lodge a complaint, partly because of the scandal involved, partly because at any moment Marie might return home. Where was the Crown Prince? She sent a message round to Count Hoyos's house, but the footman did not know where his master had gone to shoot.

The Countess next volunteered to make enquiries at the Hofburg. She returned to see the Baroness in the evening. The Prince was shooting at Mayerling with friends, and he was expected back the following evening for a family dinner party at the Court.

The night passed in terrible suspense, without any sign of Marie. The following morning Countess Larisch judged it prudent to retire to her place in the country. Poor Madame Vetsera was now desperate, and rushed off herself to the prefect of police. He received with considerable scepticism the version of Marie's disappearance as given by the Countess. He knew his world and asked Madame Vetsera straight out whether she could trust the Countess.

The Baroness lodged a complaint about the abduction of her daughter, although the prefect again made it clear that, if her daughter should prove to be with the Crown Prince, his men would be unable to proceed with the case.

Under the continuous strain of the suspense, Madame Vetsera became more and more desperate. She thought of throwing herself at the feet of the Emperor. She was not permitted to approach him, but managed to get an interview with Count Taafe.

The Count, who had been put on his guard by the prefect of police, advised Madame Vetsera to be patient a little longer. He was not at all sure that Mademoiselle Vetsera had eloped with the Prince. But, as he was dining that evening at the Hofburg, and the Prince was expected to be present, he would most likely hear something there.

Madame Vetsera was utterly at a loss to understand the reason of these evasions and delays. She implored the Count to speak to the Prince personally. He replied that his relations with the Prince were not such as to allow him to intrude in the slightest way in his personal affairs; and he expressed the opinion that, if the Baroness's conjectures were well founded, the only person who could speak to the Prince, and had influence over him, was the Empress. He added finally:

'If the Prince is present at the dinner tonight, my chief detective will have instructions to follow him afterward, although I am exceedingly averse to meddling in the Crown Prince's affairs.'

Another night passed without Madame Vetsera finding a moment's peace. In the morning, a letter from Madame Larisch brought definite evidence of Marie's *liaison* with the Prince. It was, therefore, certain that, in spite of the convenient doubts of the high functionaries, she had left with him. The Baroness was still without news from Count Taafe. Had he not seen the Prince the previous evening at the Hofburg? Why did he remain silent? Almost demented with anxiety and grief, she went to the Palace late in the morning and asked for Madame de Ferenczi, with whom she had a bowing acquaintance.

Madame de Ferenczi received her, after keeping her waiting for a considerable time. Count Taafe, she said, had told her of Madame Vetsera's trouble. She did not add that she had just heard the news of the tragic sequel to the flight. The Baroness implored her to obtain an audience with the Empress, which might put an end to her terrible suspense, and enable her to enlist the Empress's help in bringing back Marie and preventing the impending scandal. Madame de Ferenczi replied evasively that it was already too late, that a scandal was unavoidable, but that, nevertheless, Her Majesty would see Madame Vetsera.

With these words full of evil foreboding she went out, leaving Madame Vetsera in a terrible state of nervous apprehension.

A few minutes later, the Empress came in, deadly pale and evidently controlling herself with an effort. She went straight over to Madame Vetsera, who was making a curtsy, took her hand and said:

'Our children are no more.'

In spite of the terrible shock, the Baroness was profoundly touched by these few simple human words. Two mothers stood face to face united by the same anguish.

Meanwhile the Empress, as if entirely forgetful of herself, spoke of the dreadful effect of the blow, with all its immeasurable consequences, on the Emperor.

The Baroness left the Empress's presence so deeply moved and in such agony of mind that she did not realize, until she was home, that the Empress had given her no details of the circumstances in which Marie and the Prince had met their deaths.

But Madame Vetsera's martyrdom was only just beginning. During the afternoon, while she was expecting every minute a note from the Hofburg telling her when her daughter's body would be restored to her, a high functionary of the Court was announced. In insidious language he gave her to understand that it would be advisable for her to leave Vienna at the earliest moment; the circumstances of the Prince's death would shortly be public property, and an explosion of wrath by the populace, who adored the Prince, was to be feared.

Madame Vetsera looked at him in mute and blank amazement. He proceeded to explain that Baroness Marie Vetsera had poisoned the Prince and, subsequently, taken her own life. He also informed her that a compartment had been reserved for her in the evening train for Venice.

Almost paralysed with grief and terror, she yielded to the intimidation and left in the evening without waiting for the return of her brother-in-law, Count Stockau, who had started for Mayerling early in the afternoon. But the poor woman had presumed too much on her strength. She collapsed in

the train and had to get out at Reifling, where she spent the
night. The following morning, Thursday, January 31st, she
made up her mind to return to Vienna. She at once saw
Count Stockau, who told her what he had gathered at
Mayerling. The Prince and Marie had both been killed by
revolver bullets; it was impossible to conceive that Marie had
murdered the Prince; everything on the contrary pointed to
the Prince's having killed Marie first and himself afterwards.
He had not been allowed to go into the lodge, and the
officials in charge had refused to hand over Marie's body.

It was not until later that he discovered the object of the
infamous call of the functionary from the Hofburg on
Madame Vetsera. It had been inspired by the fear that
Madame Vetsera might go to Mayerling and claim her
daughter's body. How the official carried out his shameful
mission has been seen. It is to be hoped that he personally
was responsible for the actual methods used.

Meanwhile she was anxiously waiting for permission from
the Hofburg to proceed with the funeral arrangements. Like
the Emperor, she was a devout Catholic; like him, she longed
for the consolation of the prayers of the Church. And who
had tended her poor little one? Who had laid out her poor
body? Who was keeping watch over her in that lonely
chateau? Her heart bled when she thought of these things.

Early in the afternoon Count Stockau brought her a message from the Emperor. The Emperor had in his possession
a letter from the Crown Prince to her, but, before she would
be allowed to see it, she must give her word of honour to
return it at once to the Count who would take it straight
back to the Emperor.

She gave the required promise, and the letter was brought
to her. Only the envelope was in the Prince's handwriting.
Inside were three letters from Marie, dated Tuesday, January 29th, one for her mother, the other two for her brother
and sister.

The first ran as follows:

Dear Mother, Forgive me for what I have done. I cannot
resist love. I wish to be buried at his side in the cemetery at
Alland. I am happier in death than in life.

To her sister she wrote:

We are leaving joyfully for the life beyond the grave.
Think of me sometimes; and do not marry except for love.
I have not been able to do so and, as I cannot resist love,
I am going with *him*.

MARIE.

Do not grieve, I am happy. The country here is magnificent and reminds me of Schwarzau. Do you remember the
line of life in my hand? Goodbye once more. On the 13th of
January,[1] every year, lay a flower on my grave.

And to her brother:

Goodbye, dear brother, I will keep watch over you from
the other world, for I love you dearly. Your devoted sister.

After reading her daughter's last lines, Baroness Vetsera
enclosed the notes in the envelope and sent them back to
the Emperor. An hour later he returned them by Count
Stockau. She might keep them. The Empress enclosed for
Madame Vetsera, from the Crown Prince, a photograph of
Mayerling showing the windows of their room marked
with a cross in ink.

Count Stockau at last received permission to go to Mayer-
ing and bury Marie in the cemetery near Heiligenkreuz
attached to the monastery of that name. He must be provided with plenary powers by the mother of the deceased.
The orders necessary for the interment had already been
given to the monastery. The presence of Madame Vetsera at
the funeral was prohibited. The Count was expressly forbidden by the Hofburg to take either a coffin or a shroud.

[1] The date, as has been seen, on which she gave herself to the
Prince.

He was to proceed from Mayerling to Heiligenkreuz in the carriage in which he travelled from Vienna. No priest was to accompany him. He would find a coffin and shroud at the mortuary of the cemetery at Heiligenkreuz. A commissioner of police would be waiting for him at Mayerling.

Madame Vetsera was crushed by the wanton cruelty of these orders. She provided Count Stockau with the necessary powers, and he immediately left by carriage with his brother-in-law, Baron Alexander Baltazzi.

It was long after dark when they reached the chateau. They rang repeatedly without getting an answer. After they had waited for over half an hour, another carriage arrived from Vienna. Slatin, member of the Aulic Council, a representative of the Grand Marshal of the Court, and one of the Emperor's physicians, Professor Auchenthaler, got out. They managed to make the attendants hear. Without delay they broke the seal on the door of the room into which Marie's body had been hastily carried the previous morning. The sight before their gaze beggars description.

Marie, almost naked, lay on the bed. She was partially covered by a heap of disorderly garments which had been hurriedly thrown over her. No one had cared for her; her eyes had not been closed; the blood that had spurted from her mouth had not been wiped away. She lay there, stiff and stark, with her head fallen forward. No one prayed beside her.

A finding of suicide was recorded, although the hole made by the bullet behind her left ear supplied irrefutable evidence that she had been shot. Her uncles were forced to sign the statement of suicide. Failing their signature, the permission for her burial would have been withdrawn; an inquest would have been necessitated, and an even greater scandal would have resulted.

Dr Auchenthaler and a servant laid out the body. They had to clothe it in the garments in which Marie had arrived at Mayerling. When it was ready, her uncles had to arm her down the stairs, as if she had been alive, and place her in the carriage waiting outside in the darkness.[1]

The two men, with Marie between them, got into the landau and left by the mountain road for Heiligenkreuz, about six kilometres away. The road was in a terrible state, and the body swung from one side to the other with the jolting of the carriage.

They were held up by the appalling weather and had to stop to rough-shoe the horses, owing to the ice on the roads. Before they reached Heiligenkreuz, Baron Gorupp, a chief commissioner of police, stopped them, got up on to the box beside the coachman and ordered him to drive directly to the cemetery, which lay at the end of an avenue of trees some distance from the road.[2]

Not until midnight was the body wrapped in its shroud, in the little mortuary, and laid in a coffin that had been hurriedly made by the convent carpenter. Part of the night was spent in the monastery in signing and registering the official

[1] Six months later, Baroness Vetsera petitioned the Emperor for permission to make use of certain official documents for compiling a booklet to reveal Marie's true character and throw a light on the circumstances of her death. The documents referred to were used by the author for the purposes of this book.

The following extract from the Emperor's reply, which was drawn up by Count Edward Paar, the Adjutant-General, and delivered to Madame Vetsera on the 19th July, 1889, shows that later he keenly regretted the measures dictated by him:

'While his Majesty deeply regrets that the arrangements made for the burial of her unhappy daughter should have wounded the feelings of Baroness Vetsera, the consternation prevailing on the site of the calamity and the extreme urgency of the decisions necessitated must be taken into account.'

[2] The report of Commissioner of Police Habrda on the burial of Marie Vetsera was found among the papers of Count Taafe and was published in the *Neue Freie Presse* of October 1922. All the gruesome details connected with the burial and the removal of the body from Mayerling to Heiligenkreuz are included in the report. Should any of the readers of this book be shocked by them, the author would point out that these things actually happened and that Marie's uncles had to endure them.

documents. The rain, the fog, and the frozen condition o.
the ground had delayed the grave-diggers. In the morning
Marie's uncles and the two police commissioners had to help
them.

The Prior of the monastery who was present, read a
prayer over the grave and gave his blessing.

Long afterward, the Baroness was granted permission to
bring her child's body back to Vienna. She did not avail
herself of it. Marie was left in the peaceful country ceme
tery, where she had at length found rest. Madame Vetsera
built a chapel in her memory. She might have inscribed on
the walls Shakespeare's pious lines slightly altered:

'Vex not his ghost: O! let him pass; he hates him
That would upon the rack of this tough world
Stretch him out longer.'